SEALED AT SUNSET

Sunset SEALs Book 1

SHARON HAMILTON

SHARON HAMILTON'S BOOK LIST

SEAL BROTHERHOOD BOOKS

SEAL BROTHERHOOD SERIES

Accidental SEAL Book 1
Fallen SEAL Legacy Book 2
SEAL Under Covers Book 3
SEAL The Deal Book 4
Cruisin' For A SEAL Book 5
SEAL My Destiny Book 6
SEAL of My Heart Book 7
Fredo's Dream Book 8
SEAL My Love Book 9
SEAL Encounter Prequel to Book 1
SEAL Endeavor Prequel to Book 2
Ultimate SEAL Collection Vol. 1 Books 1-4 /2 Prequels
Ultimate SEAL Collection Vol. 2 Books 5-7

BAD BOYS OF SEAL TEAM 3 SERIES

SEAL's Promise Book 1
SEAL My Home Book 2
SEAL's Code Book 3
Big Bad Boys Bundle Books 1-3

BAND OF BACHELORS SERIES

Lucas Book 1

Alex Book 2
Jake Book 3
Jake 2 Book 4
Big Band of Bachelors Bundle

BONE FROG BROTHERHOOD SERIES
New Year's SEAL Dream Book 1
SEALed At The Altar Book 2
SEALed Forever Book 3
SEAL's Rescue Book 4
SEALed Protection Book 5

SILVER SEALS SERIES
SEAL Love's Legacy

SLEEPER SEALS SERIES
Bachelor SEAL

SUNSET SEALS SERIES
SEALed at Sunset
Second Chance SEAL

STAND ALONE BOOKS & SERIES
SEAL's Goal: The Beautiful Game
Nashville SEAL: Jameson
True Blue SEALS Zak
Paradise: In Search of Love
Love Me Tender, Love You Hard

NOVELLAS

SEAL You In My Dreams Magnolias and Moonshine

PARANORMALS

GOLDEN VAMPIRES OF TUSCANY SERIES

Honeymoon Bite Book 1

Mortal Bite Book 2

Christmas Bite Book 3

Midnight Bite Book 4

THE GUARDIANS

Heavenly Lover Book 1

Underworld Lover Book 2

Underworld Queen Book 3

FALL FROM GRACE SERIES

Gideon: Heavenly Fall

NOVELLAS

SEAL Of Time Trident Legacy

All of Sharon's books are available on Audible, narrated by the talented J.D. Hart.

ABOUT THE BOOK

SEALs Don't Poach on another Team Guy's girl.

Navy SEAL Andrew Carr needs a lot of mindless beach time as he comes home from his first deployment. He visits a friend he met in BUD/S at a small Florida coastal town. But what he finds is something he cannot have: another SEAL brother's girl.

Aimee Greer is running from the stress in her life, and knows the beach, and the arms of her hot new boyfriend should do the trick. But when Andrew Carr comes to visit, she's not prepared for the explosive chemistry that develops between them.

When Carr is forced to defend her from her past, she realizes she has found the one she's been searching for her whole life.

Copyright © 2020 by Sharon Hamilton
Print Edition

All rights reserved. Without limiting the rights under copyright reserved above, no part of this publication may be reproduced, stored in or introduced into a retrieval system, or transmitted, in any form, or by any means (electronic, mechanical, photocopying, recording, or otherwise) without the prior written permission of the copyright owner of this book.

This is a work of fiction. Names, characters, places, brands, media, and incidents are either the product of the author's imagination or are used fictitiously. In many cases, liberties and intentional inaccuracies have been taken with rank, description of duties, locations and aspects of the SEAL community.

AUTHOR'S NOTE

I always dedicate my SEAL Brotherhood books to the brave men and women who defend our shores and keep us safe. Without their sacrifice, and that of their families—because a warrior's fight always includes his or her family—I wouldn't have the freedom and opportunity to make a living writing these stories. They sometimes pay the ultimate price so we can debate, argue, go have coffee with friends, raise our children and see them have children of their own.

One of my favorite tributes to warriors resides on many memorials, including one I saw honoring the fallen of WWII on an island in the Pacific:

> "When you go home
> Tell them of us, and say
> For your tomorrow,
> We gave our today."

These are my stories created out of my own imagination. Anything that is inaccurately portrayed is either my mistake, or done intentionally to disguise something I might have overheard over a beer or in the corner of one of the hangouts along the Coronado Strand.

I support two main charities. Navy SEAL/UDT Museum operates in Ft. Pierce, Florida. Please learn about this wonderful museum, all run by active and former SEALs and their friends and families, and who rely on public support, not that of the U.S. Government.
www.navysealmuseum.org

I also support Wounded Warriors, who tirelessly bring together the warrior as well as the family members who are just learning to deal with their soldier's condition and have nowhere to turn. It is a long path to becoming well, but I've seen first-hand what this organization does for its warriors and the families who love them. Please give what your heart tells you is right. If you cannot give, volunteer at one of the many service centers all over the United States. Get involved. Do something meaningful for someone who gave so much of themselves, to families who have paid the price for your freedom. You'll find a family there unlike any other on the planet.
www.woundedwarriorproject.org

CHAPTER 1

A PAIR OF green Nikes haunted Special Operator Andy Carr. He was used to dreaming about girls to take his mind off anything he wanted to forget, but this was new. It didn't make any sense to dream about running shoes. Yet, night after night, he saw those shoes lying by the side of the road, attached to skinny brown legs wrapped in the brightly-colored skirt of one of the local girls who brought them things from the village.

She was one of the ones he couldn't save.

Maybe that was why he remembered the shoes and not the girl. It was self-preservation, and he refused to dwell on it. Time for that later when he was ready to talk to someone about it. Not now.

Like crowning out of a deep blue wave, he arched up out of his mattress so fast he almost hit his head on the ceiling. The motel room was tiny, and the ceiling was shallow but much taller than the bunker they'd been holed up in on their last deployment to West Africa.

He was home, and as usual, he wanted to feel normal, and only a woman could do that. He'd gotten home two days ago, after nearly twenty hours of being jumbled and jostled in a transport plane. He let that sink in before he acknowledged he'd had another one of those dreams. It would drive half the male population insane to do that more than once in a lifetime.

He could still smell the smoke and hear the sounds of the village people, even the children playing with wooden sticks, Coke bottles and toys they fashioned from the detritus of war. Somehow the kids always played. Even after some of the worst attacks he'd ever seen, after the cessation of battle, after the smoke cleared, the children would slowly creep out into the open and begin to play.

Life moves on.

The village people wanted peace, and he knew their SEAL Team 3 mission was to try to extricate several bad guys who extorted and preyed on them. These were hired guns, mercenaries without any allegiance to their land or culture, militiamen encroaching on the docile village life coming all the way across Africa or from neighboring Nigeria. They were nothing but bullies.

Although he wanted to save the villagers, he wasn't

there to do that. He was there to pluck the bad guys from the salad bowl that was their war-torn country and get them out of the mix. And in that way, perhaps he'd save the village or help them save themselves, if that was possible.

Some of the older SEALs warned him to harden himself against some of the things he was going to see. It in no way properly prepared him. This was his first deployment, and he couldn't say whether he would be able to walk into the next mission more hardened or softer from the knowledge of what real war was all about. He'd seen the movies, and he'd been trained. He'd been counseled about how his emotions would rise up, how he would feel like taking a M4 carbine and slaughtering the bad guys instead of airlifting them to base or withholding critical medical assistance, just letting them bleed out. Why not?

But no, Andy was supposed to abide by the rules of his elite SEAL Team 3 unit.

They were not savages, after all, no matter how much anger or revenge boiled up inside.

Kyle Lansdowne, his LPO, told him that it was bum luck to have drawn this particular mission for his first. He hadn't cared. He'd been ready. He told himself that every day while he worked up to his deployment.

The day they got the call and were summoned to the Team 3 metal building at Coronado, he experienced fear. And he knew it was logical and normal to feel this way. But it didn't make it any easier.

Sitting now at the edge of the bed, he let his eyes accustom to the darkness at three A.M. It was turning out to be the most dangerous time for Andy. He'd had some rest after his fun little love dance with the green-eyed girl from the Oasis bar. She'd been willing, and he was hungry.

He knew the nightmare of the Nike shoes was going to wake him up again like it did every night. That's why, when she left close to eleven o'clock, he was grateful. The sweats on his body cooled the mixture of rage and fear that heated him from the inside out, making his mouth parched and his fingertips tingle. No reason for her to see any of that. It would scare her. He was supposed to protect innocents and do such a good job of it that they didn't even worry about the dark forces out there he was battling.

He heard the foghorns in the distance, that constant thrum he recognized as the ambiance in Coronado. Occasionally, he heard a seabird in the distance. He hoped that someday he would wake up to some soft willing arms or to the sight of a gentle backside he could study. He'd watch her come alive as the sun peeked through the window. New promise of a bright, lazy day. Someone he could spend all night with and still like her the next morning.

But for right now, all he had was the remembrance of the dream again, the shoes attached to those legs, lying lifeless by the side of the road.

He got up and splashed cold water on his face. He was grateful he couldn't see himself in the mirror. He knew he wouldn't like what his eyes reflected back to him and the message he would tell himself. It was one thing to run away from people. It was quite another to deny looking at a piece of himself.

He'd do it eventually, of course. He knew he could make it work. But he needed some time. And he needed some distraction.

Cory Phillips, his medic friend from BUD/S and Specialty School, had been picked up by an East Coast team and had deployed six months earlier with his group from Little Creek. He was a Florida native and had encouraged Andy to go with him to Team 4, even though Andy was from a little farming town in central California. He'd never spent any time on the other side of the U.S.

His friend had injured his arm in a training exercise and was healing from a full elbow reconstruction. The Navy gave him three months to get healthy before they'd decide to take him back. So of course, Cory made a beeline to the Gulf Coast, back to his old stomping grounds.

Cory'd bragged that the beaches in California

weren't anything like Florida's picture-perfect, deep white sugar sand beaches and blue waters slicing the horizon. Cory told him about all the fishing and surfing they'd do. He told him they could stuff themselves on the fish they could catch off the many piers and on the shore. Live on the water if they wanted.

But when his buddy came home from the Middle East, even before his accident, he sounded different. Now that Andy had a deployment, he knew. Cory was probably also haunted by something, though probably not green running shoes…

The text message he got from him last week, complete with a picture of the beautiful nearly abandoned sugary beach on the Gulf, was damn tempting. And it didn't reflect any of the dangerous pauses and gaps in their conversation he had with Cory a couple of months ago. That had scared him.

Luckily, he had to cut the call short, because they were leading a small party into the bush. He'd been glad to be with his brothers on the mission that day because he didn't want to think about what he heard in Cory's voice. Those kinds of questions and concerns were never to be spoken over the phone. They had to be done in person.

The picture and the text message indicated he'd met a girl. He told Andy all he was going to do was savor the waves and the sun, chill at the tiki bars, and enjoy his new girlfriend, Aimee.

Andy thought maybe he'd give him a call and see if the invitation was real. It underscored what he told himself several days in a row—that the distraction would be good for him. Besides, he'd never seen Florida. And, okay, maybe he wanted to be able to prove Cory wrong. There was no way in the world Florida beaches could rival any of California's. He'd bought his ticket and was leaving for the Gulf Coast today before he had time to change his mind.

He knew sleep was impossible, so he took a shower and dressed. Stuffing clothes into a small duffel bag with the Bone Frog logo on it, he packed up his instant shakes and some energy bars he liked and headed for the airport. On the way, he would search for an all-night diner to grab some breakfast. With any luck, he'd be able to sleep on the plane. A couple Bloody Mary's would help in that department.

After an uneventful flight, Andy picked up his rental car at the Tampa airport and followed directions west toward St. Pete's, on his way to Sunset Beach.

Growing up in the San Joaquin Valley, he remembered being about ten years old when his dad first drove him to the coast where he played in the surf. It was an instant love affair, and he still could smell the salt, hear the birds, and feel the relief after clearing his ears of the sandy water from a spill bodysurfing. He respected the powerful forces of the ocean, and his dad warned him about the undertow occurrence and sometimes jellyfish he'd have to avoid stepping on.

That day with his dad, just the two of them, changed his life forever. He knew there was something about being in the water that would always be a part of his life.

His dad still operated a small farm, and both he and his mother worked long hours. Vacations were infrequent, and it was another five years before he saw the beautiful Pacific Ocean again.

But when he reported to Coronado after his Basic Training and Corps School in Michigan, he'd felt like he'd come home. That year, as they completed their further SQT, they spent time in Alaska and Mexico and had some big desert runs in Nevada. Then they'd return home to Coronado. He vowed never to live in a farming community inland away from the water again. He found swimming easy, the lifestyle in the San Diego area to his liking. The weather was temperate and sunshine nearly every day. And even in the wintertime, it felt like early spring in the valley.

Today, as he drove his rental car over the long bridge that led to the coastal towns of St. Petersburg, Redington Shores, Madeira Beach, Treasure Island, Indian Rocks Beach, and Sunset Beach, he was struck by all the water. Green tangled foliage made its way down to the water's edge. Coastal waterways linked together subdivisions of homes that fanned out everywhere on the water, almost making them look like terraforms on Mars. Huge homes rose up out of the foliage like crystals. He'd never seen so many private boats of all sizes and shapes. Unlike Southern California, he found more boats than swimming pools as he drove down the expressway ending in a dead end at Gulf Boulevard.

He turned right.

He instantly loved the beach vibe. The bright blue sky seemed bigger here. The weather was warmer. Large marshmallow clouds swept across the horizon as he glimpsed blue coastal waters between motels, condos, and restaurants. Enclaves of smaller homes and cottages were interspersed between the commercial buildings and occasional high-rises.

The cat-and-mouse game of hide-and-seek with the Gulf waters felt like he was chasing a pretty girl with big blue eyes who was playing coy and hard to get. He nearly rear-ended the car in front of him while craning his neck, peering between two large homes on stilts, built right on the ocean.

His phone GPS told him he was about five miles away. His telephone rang.

"Hey, asshole, where are you?" Cory sounded like he was extremely inebriated.

"I'm here. Just hold your knickers a bit. I think I'm about five-no, four—miles away."

"Okay okay Andy. I'm putting the steaks on now. They should be ready when you get here."

"You need anything? Do you want me to stop and get some beer or something?"

"No. Got it all. Even have apple pie thanks to Aimee. And I got enough whipped cream and vanilla ice cream to slather all over everything. So you just get your butt over here. We'll stuff ourselves, have a chat, and then I'm going to take you out to watch the sunset."

"Sounds like a plan."

The traffic slowed to a snail's pace under the late afternoon sun. In ten minutes, Andy's GPS indicated Cory's location was on the left. He waited for traffic to go by and then turned down the small alleyway bordering several brightly colored cottages arranged with a common yard. A two-story apartment complex sat farther down the alleyway. On the left side was a massive three-story home with a roaring fire pit in the front yard overlooking the beach.

Andy noticed a parking space designated for the address Cory had given him and pulled in. Before he could get his suitcase out of the car, he heard Cory yell, "Andy! Over here."

A gravel driveway, made with crushed white stones

and shells, crunched under his feet as he hoisted the duffel over his shoulder and walked several paces to his waiting friend. Cory wore a red apron with a bright orange lobster screened on the front. Underneath the lobster where the words *'Don't kiss the cook. He bites.'*

And he was nearly falling down drunk.

With a beer in one hand connected to a forearm encrusted in a bright purple cast extending from just above his wrist to within two inches above his elbow and a large stainless steel spatula held in the other hand, Cory stumbled in place. Andy saw that his assessment of his BUD/S buddy was accurate. Cory could hardly stand up. He swayed from side to side, and after a brief hug, Andy was careful to make sure his buddy was firmly planted on his feet before he released him.

"Looking good, my man," Andy lied.

"So what do you think?" asked Cory.

"Pretty fucking nice, you asshole. But I still think you're lying through your teeth about the beach. I like the weather, though. So far pretty nice."

"Just you wait."

Andy was invited into the single-story, concrete block modest home bordering the Gulf. A large picture window in the living room revealed a spectacular view of the beach and the blue water beyond. Andy noted that there was only one couple walking hand-in-hand along the surf line. He was dismayed that the rest of the beach was completely empty.

Cory appeared next to him. "Pretty nice, isn't it?"

"This definitely does not suck." Andy put his arm around Cory's shoulder, stabilizing him. "You burning the steaks?"

"Oh, hell yeah. I get distracted by this view every day," Cory said as he pointed with the spatula. He finished his beer, picked up a dinner plate from the kitchen counter, and motioned for Andy to join him on the patio in the front yard.

Andy counted three huge steaks loaded on the plate, precariously balanced on the cast. "So where is she?" Andy had to ask.

"Aimee went to go pick up a friend. Thought you might like to have some female company tonight." Cory wiggled his eyebrows up and down.

Andy felt his cheeks warm. "Well I guess I can tolerate that. So tell me about her."

"I'll let you introduce yourself. She's standing right behind you."

Andy hadn't heard the two girls arrive. As he turned, he saw two shapely mid-twenties beach ladies in cutoff jeans and oversized T-shirts. The blonde wore a ponytail sprouting out the back of her baseball cap. The brunette smiled at him with deep lavender eyes.

She extended her hand.

"Hi. I'm Aimee. Cory has told me a lot of fun things about you. It's nice to finally meet the legend."

Andy glared at his friend. "Fun things? What kind of fun things?" he asked.

Cory just shrugged and disappeared into the kitchen, mumbling something Andy couldn't understand. He turned back to Cory's girl, aware that it was a very bad sign that he couldn't take his eyes off her. He suddenly wished he was a legend or could miraculously disappear like a superhero. Or he could have a redo of the introduction. He stepped forward.

He felt the earth move as he took her hand and shook. He also smiled at the pretty blonde standing next to her, who was attractively shy.

"Nice to meet you both," he said, his voice cracking like a prepubescent teen. "Maybe you don't know it, but Cory's one of the biggest liars I've ever met."

They all laughed, even as Cory protested.

"Anyhow, he's a really good friend and a super guy." He tried to direct his conversation to the blonde but kept coming back to Aimee. He shrugged. "I guess I don't have to tell you that."

In spite of himself, he blushed. Cursing internally, he purposefully bit his lip to remove the fantasies his brain was torturing him with. Those lavender eyes were peering straight down into his soul.

The blonde, who had introduced herself as Shelley,

mercifully helped him out.

"Aimee says you're also a SEAL. Is that right?" Her cute upturned nose and inquisitive blue eyes were a welcomed relief. He searched for something about her he could find distraction in. He decided he liked the shape of her ears, and the wispy strands of hair around her forehead. Her pink cap read, 'St. Pete.' He also loved her faint Southern accent.

"I am. Went through initial training with Cory. That's how we met. But I'm stationed in Coronado, on the West Coast."

"I love San Diego," she said, her eyes widening. "I wanted to go to school there but wound up at Florida State. That made my mamma happy."

She followed it up with a smile, and Andy was enchanted.

"You *sound* like a Florida girl," he whispered.

He took a step back because he was beginning to feel like he'd never been around women before. Cory was giving him a goofy grin behind the two ladies as he placed the steaks on the table.

"Let's eat before these get cold," he slurred.

Aimee pulled a salad from the refrigerator and asked him if he wanted wine or beer.

"Um, wine, please," he said as Cory pointed to a chair next to him.

"Wine, it is then. Shelley?"

"Please."

Aimee disappeared into the kitchen one more time, rounding the counter with a bottle of red wine and three glasses. She handed Andy a wine opener.

"Care to do the honors?" she asked. Her lavender smile gave him a sizzle down his spine.

"I'm terrible at that," he muttered, watching her put the bottle on the table next to the three wineglasses.

"Really?" she mocked. "A California boy who doesn't open wine? How do they let you live there?"

He glanced at Cory, who was engrossed in carving up one of the steaks for the ladies. Andy watched him carefully, ready to grab the knife from him before he cut an artery. Cory finally mastered the cut and plopped a half on each of the two other plates and gave himself and Andy the remaining two full-sized steaks.

"Yeah, Andy. How do you manage that?" Cory mumbled.

Before he could stop himself, he answered, "I buy wine in boxes or cans."

While Cory's jaw dropped, Aimee pulled the cork out of the bottle with a loud pop, which made Shelley jump. It slipped from her fingers, and as she bent to pick it up at Andy's feet, he gasped.

She wore green Nike running shoes.

CHAPTER 2

Aimee and Shelley rinsed off the dishes and put away the remnants of dinner while Cory grabbed another beer, handed one to Andy, and agreed to meet the girls out at the beach to watch the sunset.

"He's cute, Aimee. Does he have a girlfriend, or do you know?" Shelley was drying the large plates, placing them back in the cabinet.

"I honestly don't know." Aimee had been wondering the very same thing. "You know how Cory is." She brushed her hair from her face with the back of her hand, clutching a bottle brush in her fingers.

"Oh, I get you."

Aimee continued. "He doesn't volunteer much about his friends, or anything for that matter."

Shelley sighed. "I always forget that about guys." She walked to the living room window as Aimee watched her study the pair of SEALs.

"They're all like that, Shelley. It gets worse when

they're together."

"My mom tried to fix me up with somebody from Little Creek. It was one of her biggest mistakes. I mean, we had absolutely nothing in common." Shelley wrapped her arms about her upper torso, swaying. "But oh my God, he was built," she added rolling her eyes.

Aimee hung up the towel and joined her. "I don't even know if I do or don't have anything in common with Cory," she said. "We just have fun. We laugh a lot. He's always the center of attention at any party, or bar. When we're not driving around or having a tickle fight or walking on the beach or other things," she said, closing her eyes, "his favorite thing is watching movies and eating popcorn." She felt a pang of sadness as she whispered, "And I like him better when he's not had too much to drink."

"Can you imagine what they carry around with them, though?" Shelley tipped her head to the side until the two friends touched foreheads. "And were you really looking for *forever*?"

Shelley had a knack for getting right to the point. She'd managed to bring up something Aimee had purged from her mind. "Very astute." She sighed. "I think right now, it's perfect. I don't want to have to work hard at anything. It's been a long year. Mom's at peace, and now I'm free. I don't want to make any plans. I just want to enjoy the beach and the sun."

She watched the two men splash each other in the surf and generally adopt pre-teen behavior. Being here was healthy. This was good for her. She could see Andy was good for Cory, too.

"Are you ready?" Shelley whispered.

"Let me grab a jacket and some waters. Unless you want wine?"

"No, thanks. Water's great."

The sun had just begun to touch the blue horizon. Within minutes, it began to melt like an orange popsicle. Cory wrapped his uncasted arm around her waist when they approached. She felt coolness from his soaked shirt but didn't complain. The smell of the saltwater on his skin was soothing.

No one said a word for several minutes as they stood in hushed reverence.

At last, Cory spoke.

"Well, Andy, my friend, this never ever gets old. I can remember wondering when I was a kid if there was some way I could grab and harness that sun. It looked to me like a great big golden cookie. I was sure it tasted heavenly."

"Butterscotch. That's what it looks like to me," Andy commented.

"So how long before you grab a flight back to San Diego?" Cory asked.

"I got two weeks starting tomorrow."

This was longer than Aimee thought.

"I think that's perfect. But you can stay longer, if you want to, right?" asked Cory.

Andy showed his wide smile and sparkling eyes. "All depends on how you feed me, brother."

"No worries there. And Aimee here will keep us stuffed with berry pies," Cory added, kissing her on the cheek.

The two couples sat down about five feet from the surf. Aimee sipped her water, leaning into Cory's muscled frame. He stretched his purple arm around her shoulder and gave her a careful squeeze.

"Happy?" Cory asked.

"What's not to love here?" She felt him tighten his grip on her shoulder then lean in and place another gentle kiss on her lips. She melted under his tenderness and felt her toes tingle.

"You?" Aimee asked, while watching the golden sunset splashing over all their faces.

"I got everything I need. I got my girl, I got my best friend, and I got my beer." He leaned forward and addressed Shelley, who was sitting on the other side of Andy. "I got Shelley here, too. Can't forget Shelley."

Shelley nodded and then smiled, her beautiful white teeth glowing in the sunset.

"I got my beer," Cory continued, holding up a

nearly empty bottle. "I got this beautiful white beach. *We've*," he corrected himself, "we've got this beautiful beach practically to ourselves."

Andy had been fixated on the setting sun. He inhaled. "I think that's just about the prettiest thing I've ever seen. I don't like to admit I'm wrong, but I got to say I think you're right Cory. This *is* Paradise."

"Yep." Cory clinked bottles and finished off his beer.

The four of them sat in silence, watching until the sun's dying fireball extinguished into the water. Overhead, the blue sky began to darken, turning shades of deep peach and purple.

"Look, Cory. The sky is about the color of your cast." Aimee pointed out.

Cory pulled her closer. "Did I ever tell you about that beautiful girl I saw in the yellow bikini one day who had the most awesome lavender eyes?"

Aimee was embarrassed, looking down between her knees as he fondled strands of her hair between his fingers. Finally, she looked back up at him. "Yes, but I love hearing it over and over again."

"Ahh, Cory, I never took you for a romantic," giggled Shelley.

"I can play nice." His eyelids lowered as he drew Aimee closer and whispered, "I can play *real* nice."

His kiss was deep, his tongue exploring. She was

moved by his tender display of affection. He was often so private about those things. After, she put her head on his shoulder, and he wrapped his arm around her, this time bumping the back of her head with his cast.

"Oops. Sorry." His eyes were playful and she knew his desire was growing.

"Okay!" Andy stood up abruptly. With his hands in his pockets, he shrugged. "Shelley, let's you and I go back to the house. Otherwise, I'm gonna watch something I will have a hard time getting out of my mind."

"I understand completely," she said and took his hand.

"Oh hell. Let's all go inside." Cory stuck his bottle in the sand, sprung to his feet, and gave her a left hand up. He picked up his empty bottle and proceeded toward the direction of the house.

Andy bent forward, addressing both of them. "Tomorrow morning, I'd like to take a run down this beach at sunrise. Is it very crowded?"

Cory shook his head no. Aimee added, "Never crowded at all in the morning. We get more people here at sunset, but tonight, I don't know where everybody is." She smiled at Andy and continued, "I do it all the time, just about every morning, unless I'm here."

Aimee was grateful he wouldn't be able to see her embarrassment. They walked several steps farther, approaching the weathered wooden bridge that lead over the sand dunes en route to Cory's backyard.

"I did not know that, sweetheart," Cory whispered. Then to Andy he continued. "She lives just down the beach about—what would you say, hon?—a half mile."

"I think it's easily half a mile," she answered. "It's perfect. Paradise."

The four of them made it to the backyard two by two. Cory asked Andy to help him put firewood in his poor man's fire pit, which was a large dented barrel cut in half. She'd spent several warm fall nights there roasting marshmallows and watching the stars while lounging in two bright yellow Adirondack chairs.

"I'll go get some pillows," she said.

Shelley followed her inside. Aimee pulled the patchwork quilt off Cory's bed, and picked up four beach-themed pillows from the front room couches.

Outside, she handed pillows to everyone and then slapped her forehead. "Oh darn, Cory. I forgot to get the marshmallows."

"No worries. We got pie. How about you bring that out?" Cory answered.

Andy dumped his arm full of wood next to the fire pit, arranged new wood onto glowing coals, then looked up at her. "Way better than marshmallows. It's my most important food group," he added.

Aimee danced back into the kitchen, cut the pie into quarters, and then halved the quarters again. She carried out the apple pie and cutting spatula, along with four small plates.

"Okay, so who wants a quarter and who wants an eighth?" She held her spatula up expectantly. Cory and Andy shared a glance between them and both shrugged.

"Honey," Andy said with a grin, "I'll take the biggest piece you'll give me."

BEFORE CORY FINISHED his pie, he brought out his favorite bourbon. Aimee declined, but Shelley had a pinch and then another two. While the men finished their huge pieces, the rest of the bottle was consumed. Shelley began to yawn. Andy brought more wood and spread the coals evenly one more time.

Aimee watched the snapping fire splashes levitate into the night's sky. No one said a word.

It didn't take long before Cory fell asleep, snoring loudly.

"Andy, can you help me get Cory into the bedroom?" Aimee asked.

Before she could stand, Andy scooped Cory in his arms and effortlessly carried him into the house. As she followed behind, he dropped him on the bed. She removed his shoes but left his socks on. She folded the sheets and comforter over on him.

"So Cory is done. I'm going to take Shelley home,"

Aimee told him.

Andy tilted his head, peering down at her. "Do you want me to?"

"No. I think what I'll do is take her home and then I'll let the two of you turn in for the night, okay?"

"You up for a run in the morning?" he asked her.

Her pulse quickened. "I thought you'd never ask." She liked the way it felt to smile at him. "You think you can make it at six-thirty?"

"You meet me here?"

"I'll come down the beach from the north, and if you're out you can join me. If I don't see you I'm gonna let you sleep."

"You got it, Coach," he said.

Shelley took Andy's hand and shook it. "It was really nice to meet you, Andy. Maybe we'll see each other again."

"I'll make a point of it, Shelley," he answered. Then he turned to Aimee. "You're sure I can't help take Shelley home?"

"Thanks a bunch. But I really need to get back to my own place. And Cory is out for the count, so I'm not needed here. Otherwise, I'd hang around a bit. But you've got two weeks, and I'm out of a job, so I'm pretty sure we'll be doing this again."

He extended his hand, and she found herself enjoying his gentle but extremely firm handshake.

The two girls drove in silence for the first few minutes. Shelley sighed then adjusted her seat back.

Aimee wished they had spent more time together, the four of them. She guessed Shelley felt the same.

"I can tell you like him. You don't have to hide it from me, Shelley."

Shelley shook her head. "Man, they don't make guys like that very much anymore, do they?"

Aimee agreed completely.

"You could have let him take me home, you know. I mean, it wouldn't have been the end of the world. You could have still gone home to your own place," she said, glaring at Aimee.

"So you're pissed at me, then?"

"Something like that."

"So why didn't you say something?" Aimee could see Shelley was struggling.

"Well, I am a year older than you are, Aimee. I really don't need protection, especially from that guy. Just think about it from my side."

Aimee felt like a chump. "I'm really sorry, Shelley. I hadn't even considered that. Next time, tell me, okay?"

"Thought about it. I'm not desperate. I didn't want to look that eager."

"So I think you played it perfectly, then. And I'll be sure to let him take you home the next time."

"Just as well. My place is a mess tonight. But

dayam. Did you see those arms? And the way he shakes your hand? We don't have enough of that around here." Shelley wrapped her arms around herself and humphed, lazily glancing out the windshield.

"Maybe you should move up to Virginia. Or I'll make sure Cory invites some of his other friends from Little Creek down here. How about that?"

"Wouldn't that be nice? Are they mostly like that, Aimee? The one my mom hooked me up with was an animal. I don't need any of that. I want a gentleman."

"Shelley, you're only twenty-eight. There's plenty of time."

"I'd like to find someone before I need a wheelchair and have to go trolling in senior complexes."

"See there, you're in the right place," Aimee giggled. "I'm going to remind you when you find The One. Don't worry about it. It will happen, trust me."

"You and Cory?"

"Already asked and answered. Not saying anything more."

"Sorry."

After several more minutes, Aimee turned into Shelley's neighborhood. Shelley was beginning to gather her things.

"I can't understand how a guy that nice and that good-looking doesn't have a girlfriend. It just makes no sense whatsoever."

Aimee slowed down. "Oh geez, Shelley. Now I have to go on a fishing expedition?"

"Just find out what you can, and then don't worry about it. I'm a big girl."

"Will do." Aimee asked if Shelley would like to spend the night at her place, but her friend declined. "I should have asked you before we got all the way over here."

"He has that effect on you too?"

"Absolutely not." But Aimee wasn't convinced that was the truth.

"I have to be at work at eight o'clock, and it's just easier if I leave from home. I don't wanna show up at school in my cutoffs."

Aimee nodded. She let Shelley off in the parking lot to her apartment complex and waited until she was inside the lobby, the door closed. They shared a wave, and then Aimee was on her way to her own place.

FIRST THING SHE did when she arrived home was pour a tall glass of ice water and take it outside, sitting in her two-person swinging loveseat. She began rocking back-and-forth, enjoying the squeak of the springs, the sounds of the surf, and the appearance of stars peeking through a light fog coming off the Gulf.

She stopped long enough to take two large gulps of the cold water, kicked off her shoes, and pulled a blanket around her shoulders.

SHE WASN'T REALLY tired, but if she was going to get up at six o'clock for a run, she needed a good rest. She wondered if her parents ever sat on Sunset Beach like she was right now.

It has been a great adventure to come here. It was fun getting lost every day, learning about the area, finding her perfect little beach cottage to rent. Everywhere she went, she wondered if her mom and dad had been there. Did they stroll down the same beach or eat at the same seafood dive? She almost felt as if they were still here, watching her every move.

The swing's steady heartbeat, punctuated by the rushing sounds of water and the hiss of the white spray left behind and soaking into the sand, made her feel hopeful. It was like she had come home, finally, to a place she could relax.

She could barely make out the shadow of a lone bicyclist riding down the beach in a fat tire contraption under the moonlight. She considered searching for a bicycle with balloon tires so she could do the same.

Moonlight shimmered on the water as a seagull called. She was at peace on this night, as if an old painful chapter had been completed, and a new one was about to begin.

She wasn't going to try to control it, direct or evaluate it, or even study it for too long. She was just going to let it calm the anger and pain in her soul, wash over her like the surf, claim her, and then drag her out to sea forever.

CHAPTER 3

ANDY WAITED AT the surf's edge. The sun was barely up, but it still felt wonderful on his back, compared to those wet-n-sandys they used to do at Coronado at midnight during BUD/S. There was no breeze coming off the Gulf. A fine mist was lifting, emerging from the spray and the waves beyond.

He turned to his right and saw a pickup truck smaller than a postage stamp in the distance. There were single runners, pairs of runners, and a group of older women in sweats chatting away doing a light jog as a group. They all waved and greeted him with warm smiles.

Finally, a slim woman's figure emerged from the mist. When he saw the green shoes, he knew it was Aimee. He rose to greet her.

So she wouldn't have to stop, he blended in and ran at her side. "Good morning. You were right. It's nice this time of day. A little dark, but nice nonetheless."

Her cheeks were flushed, and her light caramel colored hair stuck in dark ringlets about her face. She wore a lavender-colored zip-up fleece top nearly the same color as her eyes.

"Morning, stranger. Glad you made it. How's your head?" she answered.

"I'm fine. Really *fine*. I drank a whole bunch of water last night before I turned in. That always helps. Except for the fact that I had to get up like ten times to go pee, I slept like a baby."

She chuckled at that. "Welcome to my world. I'm the same way."

They ran in silence for several minutes. Walkers, beachcombers and two young men with metal detectors, passed them along the way. Other beach runners waved as they moved in the opposite direction.

"Can't believe how friendly everyone is," he said.

"I noticed the same when I first moved here. You meet all kinds of people on the beach too at sunset. I think here everyone's used to people coming from all over the world. Snowbirds come down from the north. It really gets crowded after Christmas. But it's just a couple of hours from the theme parks, and for some reason, there are a lot of people from Russia and the Balkan countries who visit. There's quite a community here. I have no idea why that is."

"Interesting."

Two silver-haired older men leisurely rode their fat tire bicycles toward them. As they got closer, Andy heard the gentle whir of a motor.

"Now that's smart. I like that a lot."

Aimee smiled. "There are rental places all over the place. You can also rent golf carts. Those with the fat tires are made for beach riding. They don't allow any vehicles on the beach, except the garbage crew. I'm surprised they haven't been stopped. But pedal power, that's the bomb."

She took a long drag on her water bottle and then replaced it in the pocket sewed into the back of her lavender jersey.

"You try to run every day?" he asked.

"I *try*. But I don't stress about it. Sleep is kind of delicious too. But I honestly think running keeps me from getting sick. And I feel so much better afterwards."

"I get you there. Nothing better than a good workout." He decided not to mention that he and Cory had planned on doing a couple of five-mile swims in the warm Gulf of Mexico during his vacation.

She checked her watch. Her eyebrows shot up. "Do you wanna run another ten minutes or so?"

"I'm easy." Andy cursed himself for saying so. But it was the truth, after all.

"I had to struggle at first to get into the running. I

didn't start until graduate school. And I was so incredibly slow. But I learned to be patient. And now I love it."

Andy studied the variety of housing that overlooked the beach. They had easily passed through several different sleepy beach towns. Two- and three-story condos or apartments dotted the coastline here and there. Occasionally, there would be a vacant lot or two, and several small shacks were being torn down and converted into huge concrete modern multi-million dollar homes. It was a mix of affordable and unassuming old Florida, and pretentious living in a house that matched the grandeur of the view.

As the sun rose higher in the sky, the heat began to climb. His shirt was drenched, and his running shorts had bunched up, giving him a nice wedgie he didn't want to pick. It should not matter to him about that, but it did.

Aimee slowed down and walked in long strides, looking down at her feet as she did so. He matched her deep inhale and exhales to start their cooldown.

"Wow!" she said. "I liked that. Thanks for the company."

"That was fun. Now what do we do?" he asked.

"If you like, there's a great breakfast place across Gulf Boulevard. They specialize in seafood omelets and homemade biscuits. If you join me, I'll pay. You can even have my potatoes."

Those lavender eyes were going to kill him. She was a true classic beauty. No makeup in sight, just a fresh, healthy face. He found a twinge of envy directed at Cory and immediately stuffed it down. One thing was as true now as it always has been on the Teams. If she dated another brother, that meant she was hands off. He adjusted his attitude, checking himself just to be sure he had his bearings. He knew from BUD/S that Cory could be a hothead sometimes, and he got situations wrong occasionally. Andy had busted up more than one skirmish during their training. In class, if anyone was going to get into trouble, it would be Cory. Andy vowed to make sure his friend didn't start to wonder about his loyalty.

But damn, she was honestly hard not to look at and so very pleasant to be around.

He justified that, since Cory was probably not gonna rise anytime soon, he could sneak some good dark coffee, biscuits, and a seafood omelet. No problem with that, he told himself.

And he could enjoy the view, as well as the view of the ocean.

"You're on, Aimee. Just point me in the direction of those biscuits. California makes them like hockey pucks."

Her green Nikes scampered over the sand dunes.

She had better traction, and he actually had to work to keep up with her.

They found themselves in a narrow alleyway lined in pavers between two large buildings. Palm trees planted long ago were threatening to crack the foundations of both buildings, but because they'd gotten so tall, the fronds gave a gentle cover. It was like walking on a paved jungle path.

Finally, he found himself at the edge of a familiar street.

Gulf Boulevard. It snaked through over ten little beach towns on the peninsula.

Aimee turned right, and they stood in front of a tiny vintage-decorated mom and pop restaurant.

"They only serve breakfast and lunch. It's not fancy, but you'd have to travel fifty miles to find another place that has a better breakfast," Aimee told him.

"I'll take your word for it," he said as he opened the front door for her.

They were seated up front at the painted window. Someone had drawn fish, shells, mermaids and lobster in bright colors. All of the images hovered in a circle around the name of the place:

Connie's.

Andy switched seats, since they placed him next to Aimee. That would leave his back to the window, which was something he never did.

"I got a thing about being able to see the entrance and the exit." He shrugged and continued. "It's a habit now."

"Sometimes it's so noisy you can't hear unless you're sitting right next to the person. But we're early, so all's good."

Andy accepted a small tumbler of fresh-squeezed orange juice and a pot of French press coffee for two. He opened the sticky plastic menu and was dazzled by the fact that their omelet list was single spaced, covering both pages. He scanned to the bottom.

"Eighty-four?"

Aimee smiled. "You know the funny thing is I think I've eaten here about fifteen times. I always scan the menu, but I always order the same thing."

"So what's your favorite?" he asked.

"Number thirty-five. Crab, shrimp, mozzarella cheese, black olives and sour cream, with a slice of avocado on the side."

She had an honest face, delivering her line without a smile, totally confident. He wanted to ask her a lot of things, but he decided it was safest to let her talk without his prompting.

Buttermilk biscuits were to die for. He slathered his with butter and orange marmalade. Aimee broke her biscuit in half and ate the bottom, softer side without anything extra.

"Cory showed me this place," she began. "He said his parents used to take him here when he was in a high chair."

Andy scanned the room, noting the framed pictures covering the wall up front. Various celebrities had left autographs behind. He recognized several baseball players, a couple of football players, and a row of Little League teams that Connie must've sponsored. Several country stars posing with their guitars had also eaten here.

"Looks like all the best and the brightest come here," he said. "Now, if the omelet tastes as good as this place smells, I'm gonna be okay."

Andy ordered the same thing. Aimee instructed the waitress to leave all her potatoes on his plate.

"Thanks. I'll just waddle home, Aimee."

She chuckled.

Several local watercolor artists displayed inexpensively framed pictures which were scattered everywhere. Andy picked up a flyer in a plastic stand on their table and learned about a local gallery where several of these artists displayed their work. On the backside of the brochure was a map and a picture of a calendar, each month featuring a different brightly-colored beach cottage and all by a different artist.

"We have a lot of retired here," said Aimee. "There's a book club that meets in one of the rooms off

City Hall, if you can believe such a thing. The local vet shares a building with the post office. And the post office shares a counter with the local DMV."

Andy was beginning to get the full flavor of the community. He put the flyer back in the stand when their omelets arrived.

A pile nearly an inch thick of fresh crab meat covered the top of the omelet. "I've died and gone to heaven, Aimee. Seriously," he said as he picked up his knife and fork.

It only took him ten minutes to finish the whole thing. He was suddenly self-conscious as he looked across the table, noting Aimee had barely eaten anything. He felt like a pig.

"God, you think I hadn't eaten in a week. Sometimes workouts do that."

"I'm the opposite," she said. "I'll take this back for Cory so it won't go to waste."

Andy watched her delicately pick up the crab and nibble on small pieces of the biscuit. She was well-mannered, eating properly with her left arm resting over her napkin on her lap. In between bites she dabbed her lips. She had everything but the hat and the gloves.

She frowned. "I feel weird you just sitting there watching me eat."

"I'm sorry. Didn't mean to offend."

"Am I sloppy, or dropping food?" she asked as she wrinkled her nose and checked out her shirt in front.

"No, not at all. I like watching, as a matter fact. I was just thinking that perhaps you lost your appetite observing me shovel it in."

She giggled. Pushing her plate to the center of the table, she leaned back in her chair, poured a fresh cup of coffee, added cream, and savored a long sip.

"Cory says you grew up in California. That's where I'm from too." Aimee sipped her coffee again.

"Yeah. I grew up in the central valley in a little town you've probably never heard of."

"Try me," she challenged.

"Clovis."

She rolled her eyes and then, after looking up to the right, began to nod. "Near Fresno, right?"

"Good job!"

"Well, you did say the central valley. And I was trying to think of all the little towns I've been to. I played club volleyball in high school. We had tournaments all over California and I think I've probably spent several hot and sweaty Julys playing in some junior high school gym with no air conditioning."

"An athlete, is that it?" he couldn't help but ask.

"I tried to play in college, to offset some of my fees, but I pretty much warmed the bench. We had a couple of Ukrainian girls that were over six-three, and that limited my playing time. I gave it up sophomore year."

Andy had watched the girls play volleyball down in San Diego and noted she had the perfect slim, agile body type. With her running, he figured she could probably jump and spike as well.

"Nonsense," he said. "We have a couple of Samoan and Hawaiian teams that are always playing against each other. One we call the Smurfs. They're one of the most competitive and toughest customers to beat. They just never let the ball drop. If you play like that, all you have to do is wait for the other team to make an error, because eventually, they will."

"Oh, I've played against girls like that in high school. Yeah, they're deadly."

"One of the tournaments at Coronado, the Smurfs beat one of our SEAL Teams. That really stung."

She smiled, rimming her finger around the top of her orange juice glass.

"So what part of California?" he continued.

"Davis, near Sacramento."

"UC. College town."

"Except I really grew up in a little town a few miles west of Davis. Woodlake."

"You got me there, Aimee. I've never heard of it."

"Don't feel bad. Our downtown is two blocks in each direction. No movie theater. About ten greasy spoons, a really good steakhouse, a bakery, two ice cream parlors and about fifteen drugstores."

He must've dropped his jaw because Aimee laughed.

"Don't ask me how come, Andy."

He didn't know how to read that.

"Well, in Woodlake, the drug stores have a lot of other stuff too since we don't have any chains. They sell hair dryers, shoes, even groceries. Oh, I almost forgot. We do have a funeral parlor and, I think, about six churches."

"So you lived there your whole life?"

"My dad was a doctor and had a part-time practice. But he was a biology professor at Davis. Teaching was his real love."

"Was? As in he passed away?" Andy was hesitant to delve further.

She was not looking at him but rather stared at her coffee. Very slowly, she nodded.

"Drunk driver. He was killed instantly, but my mom lingered for over a year."

He wanted to say something but wasn't on solid footing. He tried anyway. "You've had a run of bad luck, Aimee. Just meeting you for the first time here, I would have never known all this. I'd say you're a real survivor."

She gave him a brief smile. "I wish I could say that was everything, but what sustained me was that I had a wonderful childhood. Sort of a perfect life with my mom and dad and my big brother. The first time I saw Cory, he reminded me so much of Logan."

"Family's important. At least you have that."

"Not really."

Andy braced himself for a backlash to his inappropriate choice of words. He wasn't going to do anything but listen. He would not engage, because she wasn't asking for it. There was no self-pity. He saw a strong, resilient woman who didn't need to be rescued. If he wasn't careful, he'd get sucker-punched.

But her story had already touched him deeply. It made him want to call his own parents, who were thankfully still alive and active.

She turned her head, staring out the window at passing cars. Andy could swear he began to see tears form.

"That happened about eighteen months ago. But before that, when I was still in school, Logan started to get into trouble in his teens, so we drifted apart. I really missed my older brother. He always protected me."

Andy waited. It was Aimee's story to tell but only if she wanted to. He wasn't going to pry.

"Cory knows all about it so I might as well tell you too."

"Don't feel like you have to."

She studied his face, her eyes sweeping to the top of

his head and then quickly glancing at his lips, before she smiled and poured on the steady lavender gaze that made his pulse quicken. Whatever test she had placed him under, he hoped he passed. He repeated himself.

"I sincerely mean that, Aimee. We don't have to go there."

She folded her hands together in front of her on the table. Their waitress brought another pot of French press, and she leaned slightly forward to watch the bubbles and coffee grounds moving slowly inside the glass beaker.

"My brother got into drugs and alcohol. He dropped out of high school and went on the road with a band one summer. He got arrested." She licked her lips and frowned, staring at her fingers. "My dad sent him to his first rehab when he was sixteen. And then again when he was about eighteen. And then again and again. He'd leave sometimes on his own for a week or two and then come back. He stole from my folks. He'd come home from rehab and steal my babysitting money. It was heartbreaking."

"I can't imagine how bad that must have made you feel. All of you," Andy whispered.

"I think they used their entire savings trying to get him straightened out. Logan just couldn't do it. They say it's hard when they start young. Arrests their development. I believe them."

"I'm truly sorry."

"Thank you. It gets a little easier the more I tell the story. One day, Logan left and never came back. That was about seven years ago. So when I finished college and started graduate school, my folks felt like they were done waiting for him to return. They'd tried everything. Police, private investigators, checking with the rehab places he'd visited. He was just gone. I didn't understand what it meant at the time, but I used to watch my mom search through the big picture window in our living room, just hoping he'd come walking down the street clean and sober."

"They left?"

"They moved to a little town outside of Nashville a few years ago. My dad retired early from the UC system. He got a part-time teaching job at Vanderbilt and set up a small practice being an on-call physician for several larger groups. He made house calls. Everybody loved him."

"I'll bet. Sounds like it was a calling for him."

"It really was. I was so happy they had those five years. I think they were the happiest I'd ever seen them."

Andy was feeling the blood pooling in his knees and ankles. He needed to move and get a good stretch in, so he asked.

"Can we maybe walk back? I'm getting kind of stiff,

and I need to move around a bit."

"Sure." She reached for the bill, and Andy swiped it from under her fingers.

"Mine," he said.

"But I said it was on *me*."

Her pouty face mocked anger. She threw her arms around her upper torso and stuck out her lower lip.

Andy held the slip high in the air, twirling it slightly to get the waitress's attention. "You gotta be quick. Besides, you told me yourself that you don't have a job. I do." he said as he tapped his thumb to the middle of his chest.

She started to protest again, and he stopped her by raising his palm.

"It won't do any good, Aimee. This is non-negotiable."

Andy wanted to hear the rest of the story but feared he should've stopped her, and now she was embarrassed with the reveal. If she wasn't Cory's girl, he would do something stupid like touch her shoulder or hold her hand, or something to reassure her that, with him, she was safe.

However, Aimee *was* Cory's girl, and so he kept his distance, walking behind her through the palm tree path, and onto the white beach again, where he could breathe. All the heaviness of their discussion floated away.

The morning was still on the chilly side, so no one had set up beach chairs or blankets. Everyone they passed was either walking or running, singly or in groups.

Her pace was quick, which was exactly what he hoped for. Then he remembered the omelet.

"Did you get the—"

Aimee held up the white styrofoam box in a plastic bag with Chinese characters all over it in red. "Cory's breakfast." She checked her watch again. "If he's up."

The same two silver-haired older guys had removed their jackets and rode their fat tire bikes in flip-flops and their swim trunks. He hadn't noticed until now that one of them had a short ponytail.

"I just love those things." Aimee said.

"Well, let's try to get you one. Let's rent three and go for a ride."

"That would be so much fun."

Her lighthearted comment convinced Andy she was done with the sad tale. He started examining the crushed shells beneath his feet as they walked in tandem. A pair of brown pelicans flew overhead, heading out into the water, joining another pair. They took turns circling and then plunging into the water to fill their bellies with fish.

A small fishing boat trolled through the waters past the row of red buoys, a couple of lines dragging behind.

The boat was being followed by a flock of about thirty seagulls, who fought over what must have been pieces of fish that had gotten chummed in the boat's propeller.

Aimee's phone rang. Andy recognized Cory's voice immediately.

"Wow, you're up about two hours before I thought you would. Are you hungry?" she said into the phone.

"Sorry, Aimee. I guess I wasn't much fun last night."

"I needed the rest. Andy carried you to the bed, and I took Shelley home. Anyway, I went for a run on the beach and picked up some old crusty barnacle here. We just had breakfast at Connie's, so I brought you the rest of my crab special."

She finished the call, tucking the phone in her zippered breast pocket.

"He okay?" Andy wanted to know.

"He sounds pretty damned good. It looks like today will be one of his good days." She looked up to him with a brave smile.

That look told him all he needed to know. She'd come to Sunset Beach to heal. Cory was someone she could take care of. He was consuming her entire world and helping her to forget.

Or at least trying to.

CHAPTER 4

Aimee found Cory sitting on one of his bright yellow chairs. He was sunning himself, his legs outstretched, flip-flop encrusted feet resting on the lip of the fire pit. He wore black wraparound sunglasses and was shirtless. Only thing missing was the tanning lotion.

His upper torso was packed, sculpted, and hairless. In fact, he was the most perfect-looking guy she'd ever dated. For all his casual and somewhat irreverent personality traits, staying in top physical condition was no joke to Cory.

"Hey there, sailor," she said as they opened the gate and entered the patio.

He sat upright, removing his glasses, and then scrambled to his feet when he saw Andy.

"So now you've seen Connie's, and how does it rate?" he asked.

"I don't think I've ever had a crab omelet like that

before. It was an outstanding recommendation," Andy answered.

Cory paused slightly, studying Andy's face. Then he focused on Aimee, stepping forward to present her with a tender kiss. While she went up on her tiptoes and wrapped her arm around his neck, Cory was gingerly extricating the bag from her fingers. "Thanks babe," he whispered in his sexy, private, '*for her ears only*' type of voice that gave her a tingle down her spine. She wondered what she'd done to deserve such attention.

But she loved it.

His fresh, clean-shaven cheek and tender kiss had her melting dangerously. She broke free, trying to respond as if it was bedroom talk, rubbing his left butt cheek when she whispered, "I'll go get your fork. Be right back."

As she stepped into the doorway, his words followed behind her. "I'll be right here," he called, mimicking her voice and continuing to play along.

Inside the house, she grabbed a fork and napkin. As she passed the open door to the bedroom, she discovered Cory had even made the bed. Andy's room, in contrast, was completely torn apart with the coverlet and even the sheets halfway ripped off the mattress. She smiled to herself. He was either a thrasher, or he'd had company last night.

Once outside, Cory dug into the food, devouring it in mere seconds.

"I was going to offer to heat it up, but I can see that is completely unnecessary."

He gave her a cheesy grin and completed his meal.

"Was there some sort of alien abduction here today?" she asked.

Cory's eyes danced. Andy looked completely confused.

"Whatever do you mean?" He set the paper plate on the grill in front of him, begging for her explanation.

"You straightened the bedroom. You even made the bed, Cory."

Andy leaned back in his chair and chuckled. "I didn't," he mumbled.

Cory chuckled while he brushed biscuit and egg pieces from his trunks. "I like to surprise you now and then." His grin came late, but it was still a grin.

"I like surprises very much," she purred back.

"Yes, I know that."

Andy sighed. "Just tell me now, Cory. Should I get a room somewhere? I feel like I'm getting in the middle of something."

Cory lazily leaned over in his direction. "Usually, the girl is in the middle, sport."

"Cory!" she screamed. She was genuinely shocked

at his behavior.

"It was just a joke, and I didn't mean to disrespect you, sweetheart."

Andy's puzzled expression hung in the air like an old jacket. Carefully, he leaned back, crossed his legs, and waited for anything else to happen.

She changed the subject. "Do you want some orange juice or something else to drink?"

Cory smirked and picked up an opened longneck beer bottle. "I got it," he said, holding it up.

Aimee was slightly surprised but had seen this before.

Andy interrupted, nervousness making his voice wobble. "We came up with a great idea, if you're into it, Cory. How about renting some of those fat tire bicycles so we could ride up and down the beach?" he asked.

"I'm good with that plan," he answered. "Aimee has been wanting to try one of those motorized bikes ever since she saw them. Right?"

"I think it's a great idea," said Aimee. She looked down at her running outfit. "I'm gonna go take a shower and change, if you don't mind?" She'd directed her question to Andy. "We only have one bathroom, sorry."

That brought a frown to Cory's face, and then he spoke up. "Well, instead of waiting maybe he could join you." He widened his eyes and presented both of them with a Joker grin.

"You asshole," muttered Andy. "I had to carry your fat ass to the bedroom last night. That's what kind of a fucking host you are. We did you a favor and let you sleep."

"And I thank you for that, Andy."

"Maybe I should go find a spot to hang out for a couple of days, and then we can start all over again. Act like adults."

"No, don't do that," both Aimee and Cory said in unison.

"Go take your shower, honey," Cory instructed. She rose and headed for the house. Behind her, she heard Andy address her wayward boyfriend. She turned to watch the fireworks.

"Now, about tomorrow…" Andy pointed his forefinger at Cory's face. "I'm gonna pour ice water on you and get your butt up and on the beach for our morning run. And that's going to be oh-six-thirty, Casanova. You got it?"

"Yes sir. Whatever you say, sport." Cory had lost the scary grin but sat to full attention.

Aimee wasn't quite comfortable with the swearing back-and-forth between the two friends, but she got loud and clear the message, veiled as it was, that Cory wasn't happy about the run or being left out at breakfast. She retreated to the bedroom.

As she stripped and stepped into the shower she couldn't recall picking up jealousy in Cory's nature before. But then, she'd not seen him around other SEALs very often. Maybe that was how they played, a little rough, joking as if demonstrating a lack of respect. Every minute she'd spent with him, she learned little subtle things, like how Cory liked to live slightly on the edge. He could make fun of the most ridiculous situation. Nothing, except his commitment to his Brotherhood or his manhood, was sacred. Although they enjoyed each other, she came second.

She dried her hair and dressed in stretchy jeans and a halter top so she could get full sun on her back but protect her legs from the bicycle mechanism. She applied light pink lip gloss and blotted her lips. When she dropped the tissue into the wastebasket, she noticed something.

A golden plastic pill bottle lay on its side, partially obscured by other paper garbage. She bent down to pick it up. Cory had told her he was done with the painkillers. But, unless he flushed the contents of this bottle to dispose of the unused pills, this was evidence that he'd been lying to her.

Her surprise discovery worried her. Clutching the bottle in her hand, she joined Cory and Andy on the patio.

"It's all yours." she said, pointing to the sliding glass door.

Andy jumped to his feet and disappeared inside. Cory had put his sunglasses back on and continued to soak up the sun. She picked up his plate, his now-empty beer bottle, and leaned over to speak to him.

"Hey, honey, I'm going to take this inside. But can you first explain to me what this is?" She held the bottle between her thumb and other fingers.

Cory slowly removed his glasses and sat forward. She handed it to him. He slowly studied the label, turning it like he was seeing it for the first time.

"I had one left. I took it early this morning, because my elbow is just killing me."

He didn't look at her.

"But you still had alcohol in your system from last night. And look at you now. You're drinking a beer with your breakfast," she reminded him, her concern growing.

He nodded. "I know. I'm careful. It was just one pill."

"You know I've had some experience, some history with this, and it freaks me out. Being careful isn't the point. It's a little reckless, Cory. You know better."

Cory stood, tossing the bottle onto the chair, and enclosed her in those strong arms of his. "I'm sorry, sweetheart. It was dumb. You're completely right. It ends here."

Still standing, he leaned back at the hips to study her face, placing his palms at the sides. "I know you mean well, but you don't have to worry about me. I'm *fine*." He pulled her to his chest, gently rocking the two of them from side to side. "But thanks for looking out for me just the same."

His kiss and gentleness brushed aside her niggling worry.

Andy appeared, dressed and ready to go. "You want to drive the Jeep?" he asked, holding up the keys.

"Absolutely." She took in the trash and grabbed a jacket she'd left in the closet.

On the way out to Andy's rental, she saw Cory dump the bottle discreetly in the gray garbage can at the curb.

AIMEE SPED DOWN the beach on a bright red fat tire bicycle, screaming at the top of her lungs. She tried to stay out front of Cory and Andy but didn't take as many chances as they did, as they wound around beachgoers and other obstacles.

The motor was pegged to five miles an hour which, while not very fast on the road, seemed like jet speed on the beach. The boys were reckless, swerving to avoid people, umbrellas, beach chairs, and a small group of teenagers, who chased them every time they zipped by.

On a couple of occasions when they got too close to some beachgoer and weren't sure they'd clear, Andy or Cory would just dump the bike, sacrificing themselves.

Aimee wasn't able to ride without the assist, so she maintained just enough tension to make it a good workout, without imploding her quads.

Several hours later, her ribs hurt; she had laughed so hard. The sunlight on her face and then on her back as they traveled up and down the beach felt wonderful. They maintained a five mile loop until her legs began to burn.

She stopped and Cory told her to continue to a large wooden bench a few yards north. Once she arrived, she noticed a beach access bridge with a large bench big enough for all three of them planted in the sand. The bikes were carefully laid on their sides as they caught their breath and talked to several groups of kids or curious onlookers who traveled the bridge for the day's adventure.

Cory volunteered to take the access toward Gulf Boulevard on an ice cream mission. Andy agreed to accompany him while Aimee stayed behind to guard the bicycles.

She sat still and just observed, letting her mind relax. There was something about Sunset Beach that settled her insides. The white noise from the turning waves, calling of sea birds, and the squeal of little children transported her back to her childhood and much happier days.

Mounted on the wall in her kitchen was a wooden plaque she bought in one of the local beach decor shops. It read, *The beach fixes everything.*

Sitting alone in the afternoon sun, she completely agreed.

The panoramic view in front of her was at least ten miles wide in both directions, where beachgoers looked hardly bigger than a grain of sand.

Maybe it was the salty air or the gentle wind in her face. She felt healthy, alive, freed from the pain of watching her mother lose her battle and her will for life. Everything important was in front of her, as if the past had been wiped away.

The bright orange sun was falling and would mate with the horizon in an hour. She could feel the rays warm her heart. All she came here for was distraction. Instead, what she got was her life back. She began to unthaw.

In a silent homage to the goddess of the sun and a God she knew loved her despite her flaws, she said a prayer. She was grateful, and like a mermaid who had emerged from the ocean for a life on land, she was firmly walking on two feet toward a bright future.

Her thoughts were rudely interrupted by the sight

of the scoop of chocolate chip cookie dough on a waffle cone nearly the quarter the size of her head. Rivulets of vanilla ice cream had already traveled down the outside of the cone and over the fingers of her handsome Navy SEAL.

Cory was now kneeling in front of her presenting the cone.

"Holy cow, Cory. This is huge!" she said.

Andy appeared next to him. He handed her several paper towels and gave the rest to Cory. He had a ring of chocolate around his mouth and a small spot at the tip of his nose.

"I tasted yours, Aimee," Andy said. "Feel free, I mean, if you can't finish it, I'd be happy to oblige."

"If you value your life, you'll stay out of my ice cream, Andy." She was rewarded with a bright, wide smile and a wink.

"Cory's warned me about you. And based on what I saw you doing with that bicycle, I can see you are a competitor."

"Oh, but she is so wicked when she plays cards," said Cory. He put his hand up to his mouth, forming a megaphone, and whispered, "She cheats."

"I do not!"

But Cory wasn't paying any attention to her. He was prattling on about all the card and Monopoly games she'd won.

"Not fair! I call foul!" she said. "I'm a fighter because I don't like to lose."

Both men howled, Andy falling to the ground as if he'd been stabbed. He nearly lost his double scoop.

Minutes later, she handed the rest of her cone to Andy, who accepted it gleefully. She washed her hands in the drinking fountain beside the bench, drying them on her jeans.

The sky was turning a deeper shade of blue. It had been forecasted for rain, so large billowy clouds had sprung up while they rested. As the sun dropped into the water, the clouds turned from white to various shades of purples, peaches and occasionally golden yellows.

Several groups of people had gathered on the beach to watch the sunset. Everyone was caught up in their own private thoughts, observing the death of one day and preparing for another behind it.

"Come on. Let's get home before it's too dark," Cory said. "And we have to get the bikes back to the shop before closing time at eight."

She walked between the two of them. It felt good to run this morning. Felt good to get to know Andy a little. The exercise on the bike was invigorating. She'd sleep well tonight.

"Anyone up for oysters?" Cory shouted. "We should go to JJ's. The drinks are half off until seven, and they make the best jambalaya in all of Florida!"

CHAPTER 5

THE PARKING LOT was so full that the spillover also filled the church parking lot next door. Aimee trolled the row upon row of trucks, SUVs, golf carts, small camper RVs, and sedans. There were license plates from several eastern seaboard states, as well as several from Texas, Tennessee, and North Carolina.

"I think I see one over there next to the white truck," said Andy.

It was obvious that if they made it into the space, nobody would be able to open their doors to get out.

"I'm going to give myself more space," said Aimee. "I don't need another door ding. And there's got to be someplace along the street, as long as you guys don't mind walking a bit. Or I could drop you off and find a spot then meet you inside."

"Are you nuts?" Cory squinted his eyes and looked at her disapprovingly. Andy completely agreed.

"Yeah. You're stuck with us, Aimee," he told her.

Just as she was going to head out to find another spot, a huge four-door truck with tires nearly the size of a small airplane began to leave. The windows were blackened, and it had a custom paint job with a non-stock chrome grill and fancy custom lights that practically required sunglasses. But Andy still recognized it as a Ford.

Centered in the middle of all the crisscrossing chrome and extra lighting was a set of horns about twelve inches in length, mounted wisely upside down with the tips pointing to the ground for obvious reasons.

Across the blackened windshield in oversized scripted letters was the name, *Phyllis.*

All in white.

"Holy moly, Phyllis. How the hell do you get inside that cab, sweetheart?" Cory whistled and shook his head in disbelief.

The monster truck slowly wound through the aisles of haphazard and unmarked parking spaces. When Aimee turned off the ignition, Andy heard the blast of a special carburetor system, and the squeal of those oversize tires making a huge statement. A cloud of gray smoke trailed behind without any chance of catching up.

Inside, the place was packed. Long tables with benches were set up in the middle of the room. Tables for two rimmed the outside. He'd expected they'd have to wait, but they were shown to the end of a picnic table they were to share with a party of four, two couples.

Up front, he saw a raised dais, with microphones, drums, and equipment set up for a small band.

"We're going to have entertainment tonight?" Andy asked, his voice slightly elevated.

Cory craned to sneak a look up front and then turned back to their group. "We got the Flamingo Cowboys tonight. What the hell kind of band is that?"

Aimee shrugged her shoulders. "The only flamingos I've seen with cowboy hats are cartoons."

"Probably a local band," said Andy.

They ordered three bowls of jambalaya, and then Cory ordered a dozen barbecued oysters.

"And to drink?" the waitress asked.

Cory scanned a chalkboard she pointed to and picked a local IPA. "We'll have a pitcher."

"Three glasses then?"

Aimee pointed to a picture on the menu of an oversized margarita glass filled with pink icy liquid. A long pink and white striped straw had a pinkish orange paper flamingo attached to it.

"I'll have that."

"JJ Margarita special then. Just one?"

Cory and Andy looked at each other, and Andy

spoke first. "Actually, make that two."

"Cory raised his forefinger, and asked for a sixteen ounce, instead of the pitcher.

Andy was having a hard time hearing anybody so he scanned the crowd. He didn't expect to see anyone he knew, but he'd been trained to assess any new environment. He noticed a rear door next to the kitchen entrance. Over his head, he saw at least six cameras attached to a ceiling grid that panned the crowd.

Narrow stairs lead to a short landing and a door beyond, indicating there was a small office or observation room above the kitchen. He figured it was where all the recording equipment and security detail was located, because he didn't see anyone of authority downstairs.

Cory had been searching as well. The two nodded.

The margaritas arrived, twice the size of what they looked like on the menu. Cory held his mug up, and they toasted.

"To Sunset Beach. To good friends and happy memories."

All three of them pulled on their drinks.

"Oh, I like this!" Aimee said. "Cory, you got to try mine."

Andy completely agreed. The drink was luscious and went down like fresh fruit juice.

Cory shook his head and waved her off.

"I think it's grapefruit and definitely pineapple, but I'm not sure," Andy said. "It has some Cointreau in it, too, and something else. Very smooth. I approve."

Aimee raised her glass, and all three of them toasted again.

"Out with the old and in with the new," she shouted.

"It isn't New Year's, Aimee," Cory spat back.

"It kind of feels that way to me, though. I'll just get a two-month start on it. Is that okay?"

"Whatever you want, sweetheart." Cory rubbed his thumb across her lips. "You can have Valentine's Day every day if you want it."

Andy watched Aimee blush and tried not to stare.

A table of young ladies were drinking just behind them. Andy knew immediately it was a bachelorette party. His internal radar flew into high alert. He turned when he caught two of the girls whispering and pointing in his direction.

Dammit.

Cory ordered another beer when they got their oysters and the stew. The hot sizzling barbecue and garlic butter was fantastic, and all dozen of the things were gone in a matter of seconds.

The jambalaya was to die for. It was spicy hot but not so much as to shatter his taste buds. It contained jumbo shrimp, crawdads, oysters, clams with their shells, and muscles, all in a brown okra gumbo. It went perfectly with the margarita. But he found himself closing his eyes when he drank, since the pink was distracting and didn't match what he tasted.

The band started playing, which made any kind of discussion impossible. He also knew that tomorrow on his morning run, his ears would be ringing.

Cory turned around on the bench so he could watch the band. A very tiny dance floor was located just in front of the stage. Cory grabbed Aimee's hand and pulled her through the sea of tables to join several other couples.

He watched Cory and Aimee move together. She was a good dancer, but Andy could tell Cory didn't know the first thing about leading. The combination Country and Latin beat was catchy, and before long, he noticed he'd been tapping his feet, as well as his fingers, on the tabletop.

The rest of the dance crowd were older couples, silver-haired snowbirds probably, drinking and dancing on a Wednesday night, which was likely something they never did at home. He liked the fact that the whole room of people had come from so many different places. Some were recent refugees to Florida, bailing from other high-priced areas of the country. Others were just here on vacation, escaping a blustery fall somewhere.

Aimee had told him she came for distraction. And that was probably true for all three of them.

The second set began, which was a slow dance. The older couples resumed their positions, probably used to dancing with each other for decades. But Cory and Aimee were clowning around, laughing, as Cory held her and then dipped her low to the ground and up again. They danced in a bear hug but as close as they could get. He watched her face as she leaned into Cory's shoulder and closed her beautiful lavender eyes in a daydream.

He felt a tap on his shoulder and looked up to find a very pretty, well-endowed redhead staring down at him.

"Care to dance?" she asked.

"Sure."

On their way to the dance floor, he heard clapping and laughter. Someone yelled out, "Go for Ginger!"

She stepped right up into him, her chest forming a pillow between them. He slipped his arm around her waist, directing her to an open space in the dance area, and she followed perfectly.

"Where are you from?" her orange lips asked in a soft Southern drawl.

"California. And you?"

"We are all from here. Well, almost all of us. But we

all grew up here and have been friends since grammar school."

"Ah!" he said as he looked down on her. She smiled sweetly, a little shy, but she was comfortable around men, and he liked that. She was easy to like and perhaps easy to talk to. As he gave a fleeting glance to the cleavage helped with some kind of a push-up bra, he thought probably she would be easy to fuck too.

But that wasn't really a serious thought. He could be the guy she was dared to ask, and he knew how to be a gentleman, so he would politely do his duty, help her look like a princess, and would return her to her friends.

He caught Aimee staring at him, and then she quickly glanced away. When Cory turned her around, he gave Andy a wide-eyed all-knowing smile.

"So how long are you going to be in Florida?" she asked.

"Two weeks. I have to get back to work."

"I see. Well, that means you'd be here this weekend. Would you come if I invited you to my best friend's wedding?"

He knew exactly what to say next. It was a standard answer whenever he got into situations he needed to exit cleanly. "I kind of have someone back home. I'm out here to visit my buddy." He nodded in Cory's direction.

She turned, looking at Cory and Aimee dancing. "I think he's local. Is he?"

Andy didn't want to speak for Cory, so he lied for him instead. "No, he's up in Virginia. He's just down here for some workman's comp time. Did you catch his purple cast?"

"Oh!"

Her eyes had drifted to Aimee. "Well then, I'm going to have to ask Gretchen if it's okay to invite all three of you. It's going to be a fun party. My friend is marrying Anson Moore III. You know, the Moore's who breed racehorses?"

"I'm afraid you know way more about that than I do." He paused and then tried to soften the turn down. "We have lots of plans to go fishing and do all kinds of things while we're here, so I'm afraid our days are pretty full. But thank you anyway."

She appeared to take it well. "All right." Her sweet voice washed over him, and he could feel himself get hard. He decided to just experience it, instead of trying to turn it off.

He was getting used to his arm around her waist, used to the way she blended her fingers with his, used to her subtle floral scent and the way her nipples felt brushing against his chest.

She was his for the taking. She'd be soft and loving. She'd make him feel good about himself. He'd enjoy watching her shatter beneath him. He knew he could satisfy her, and he wouldn't wake up the next day and feel dirty. But it wasn't what he was looking for.

It suddenly struck him how odd this was. The old Andy would never pass up the chance to spend a little fun time with a pretty girl.

Maybe I'm just getting old. Is this what I have to look forward to?

And then the music was over.

She held his hand, dragging him over to the table with her friends. Each time he tried to sneak a look at Cory, he was laughing. He knew there would be jokes at his expense tomorrow about getting ensnared, and fondled, even mildly felt up on his second day in Florida. He knew Cory would tell him that the girls here were beautiful. And they were.

As Ginger introduced him to the female side of the wedding party, he made a point of being courteous but not giving anyone too much attention over anybody else. He declined their invitation to join them for drinks.

"No, ladies," Ginger began. "He's here visiting his friend and his friend's girlfriend. Kaitlyn, honey, do I have your permission to invite them to the wedding?"

The bride wore a tiny white veil with miniature wedding rings, baby pacifiers, and several other flesh-colored charms he didn't recognize stitched into the veil. She looked ridiculous.

Kaitlyn, the bride, examined him as if he was a piece of meat at an auction house. She was cold as hell, but her eyes lit up when she said, "On one condition. I got to have one dance."

She opened her purse, leaned across the table and handed him an invitation to the wedding and reception. It was in two days. That's when he recognized the flesh-colored shapes sewn to her veil. They were penises.

"Obviously, you don't have to RSVP. The more the merrier," she said, the little penises bobbing with the movement of her head. Her smile was picture-perfect. Her eyes came alive when he took the invitation and stuck it in his jacket pocket.

"Thanks, Ladies" he said as he gave them an extremely shallow bow.

He got a bouquet of titters for his trouble. Cory gave him a standing ovation when he came back to his seat. Even Aimee was laughing at him.

"I can't help it if I'm irresistible."

"Damn straight. See what happens when you clean up and wear a jacket and a button down shirt?"

His pink margarita looked like a tired glass of Hawaiian punch. Even the straw was drooping, and the paper flamingo had fallen on the table. He looked over at Aimee's and noticed she had finished hers. Of course, that nice little glow at her cheeks would've told him that.

Their waitress told him he could get a refresher, on the house, so he asked to try a regular margarita with no salt on the rocks this time.

"So we got an invitation for this wedding on Saturday." He threw his thumb over his shoulder and explained, "The bride's the one with all the BS on her veil."

"Oh yes." Aimee giggled. "I see what you mean."

"Very tacky," he said.

"Shocking, even," Aimee added and then chuckled.

Cory leaned forward on his elbows. He had three empty beer glasses in front of him. "So what's the plan, Stan?"

Andy took the invitation from his jacket and showed it to Aimee and Cory. "They're all local. The bride's marrying some horse breeder."

"Oh a trophy wedding!" enthused Cory. "I love those. The old man must be ancient."

"I'm not sure." Andy tapped on the name.

"Anson Jonathan McKinsey Moore, the third?" Cory read. "Yeah, they're loaded. I think they're Pegasus Farms. He's a bigwig in local politics too. Owns a couple sports franchises—I don't know which ones." He leaned back in his chair, placing hands on top of his head and stretching to the side, and then moved his right arm up and down slowly, babying his brand new joint.

Aimee pushed the invitation back to him. "I don't think that's my kind of thing. But you guys could go."

"So let me get this straight, Aimee. You're encouraging Andy and me to go crash a wedding party with a bunch of oversexed bridesmaids and probably half the pretty girls in Florida, single and just dying to get laid by a Navy SEAL? Is that what you're saying?"

"No, of course not! I didn't see it that way. If I don't know anybody there it really wouldn't be any fun for me. I don't want to go just to say I attended some big wedding for the rich and famous. That's not really who I am."

"But why not?" he insisted.

"It would probably just be uncomfortable. I'd be so nervous I wouldn't enjoy it. That's all."

But Cory wasn't going to give up so quickly. "Let's see, they'll probably have a French chef, a Cuban chef, pastry chef, free booze, and a tribute band, that will be even better than the real guys. It says here it's at the Belle Meade Country Club in Sarasota. Now, the brief amount of time I was there—well, let me put it this way, before I got kicked out—it looked like a pretty cool place."

Andy couldn't help but chuckle. "And being totally

practical, like Cory here?" He paused while Cory toasted him. "We'll need you to drive us home Aimee."

"There's Uber."

Andy tilted his head and then began shaking it no. "She doesn't wanna go, Cory." He placed his fingers at the top of the card preparing to rip it up when Cory stopped him.

"Give me that."

"Cory, what are you doing?" asked Aimee.

"I'm here to keep you two from making a huge mistake," barked Cory. "Trust me. I'd *pay* to go to one of those functions. And we got a free ticket in. I think you could even bring Shelley, if you wanted to, Andy. I'd bet she'd love it."

"Does that change your mind any?" Andy asked her.

"You really think this is a good idea? Do *either one* of you think this is a good idea?" Aimee said as she alternated searching both their faces.

Andy knew without looking at Cory what his answer was going to be.

In unison, they both said, "Yes!"

"I gotta go pee." Aimee stood and headed toward the kitchen with the bathrooms just beyond.

"You think we just screwed up, Cory?"

"No, she'll come around. And if she still is adamant about not going Saturday morning, I'll take her somewhere. You and Shelley should go. I think it will be a good way to check out how the better half lives in Florida. I guarantee you won't ever see anything like it again."

"I'm thinking maybe the three of us should go. Less things to manage." Andy read in Cory's expression that they were on two different pages. "No, no, no, Cory. I don't mean anything like that."

"Sure you did."

"It will give us all something to dream about. Something to aspire to. Something to tell our grandkids someday." He paused. "Remember what we said? To making happy memories? Now that's what I'm talking about. What were *you* thinking?"

Cory just groaned and rolled his eyes. Andy knew that by the time they made it home, he'd be in no shape to walk. In fact, Cory would probably be asleep as soon as he hit the backseat of the Jeep.

CHAPTER 6

ALL THE WAY back to her Sunset Beach home, Aimee thought about something that happened at the restaurant. She wrestled with the idea of telling Andy but decided against it.

They'd placed Cory in the back seat of the Jeep so he could stretch out over the bench. Andy insisted he hadn't consumed enough alcohol to be impaired, so he drove. That left the passenger side for Aimee.

She was in a very light-hearted mood tonight and was headed back to their table when she noticed two men arguing in the backyard. The rear restaurant door was open, but a screen protected the inside diners from bugs. Both men were wearing white, indicating they worked in the kitchen.

One man began to shout at the taller one. He began pressing his forefinger into the other man's chest, making some kind of demand. He was rotund and shorter of the two, with black curly hair growing like weeds all over the top of his head. He even had a heavy mustache. The other man was extremely thin and much younger. He also towered over the angry man by more than six inches.

Several times, the force of the older man's chest tap became more like a small shove, causing the other one to step back. Finally, she saw the younger man hold up his hand and shout, "Don't you dare!"

The words echoed throughout the alleyway behind the restaurant and even made a neighboring dog start to bark.

Both men looked back to the screen door of the restaurant. Aimee froze in place and then noticed something familiar about the younger man. At first, it was his voice. Although he'd been pushed to anger, the basic timbre was very familiar.

She pressed close to the screen to get a clearer view and called out, "Logan?"

Both men ran in different directions. She heard a car start and another slam of a car door.

It can't be! Although she doubted the impossible, she still had to check it out.

She noiselessly unlatched the screen door, stepping out onto the paver tiles traversing the small yard. She stopped and listened again for any sound out of place and found none. Certainly there was no arguing.

She called out again, "Logan? Are you out there?

It's Aimee. If you're there, let me talk to you. You don't have to be afraid."

No one answered. And although their white jackets could easily stand out in the moonlight, she couldn't find evidence of either man anywhere.

Suddenly, her knees began to shake, and her breath became ragged. The dark night felt evil, menacing, and she ran back to the safety of the warm establishment and her two SEAL protectors.

But the encounter with the two strangers had rattled her. She'd not been sleeping well lately, so tried to justify that it was a hallucination brought on by nerves, caused by a lack of sleep. And the more she played the strange visitation over and over again, as she watched the road and let the two-lane highway lull her back to normalcy, the more she began to doubt that it had happened at all.

It certainly wasn't Logan. It couldn't be. Logan would have appeared, come up, and talked to her. No matter what state he was in, he'd never just flee without talking to her.

IT WAS THE first time in the ensuing seven years that she'd actually seen someone that closely resembled him. There had been lots of false starts over the years, people who looked like him from behind. But when she examined their faces, they were complete strangers.

She knew it upset everyone around her when these things happened. So, eventually, she made it a point not to search anymore. Her parents had moved on years ago. She adopted the same attitude.

Leaning back in the seat, she closed her eyes for a few minutes.

"You okay?" Andy asked her.

"I think I'm getting a migraine or something. My whole head hurts."

Andy pulled a water bottle from the pocket in the side of the driver door and handed it to her. "You need more water. Hydration will do the trick."

He was probably right. She thanked him and took a long swig.

She turned, pulling one knee up so she could sit sideways, and looked at his handsome face. Red and yellow lights reflected on his statuesque features. By contrast, her brother's face was very angular and sharp, and in the vision she'd seen tonight, if it was real, the features were even more so.

The last time she saw him, his eyes appeared to have sunk farther into his skull, revealing dark brown circles beneath. He still had the same prominent cheekbones, but below, his face was gaunt and the coloring was pasty white. Unlike the man she was looking at now, Logan seemed like he was near death.

"So tell me what's going on?" he asked. His deep

voice was soothing and kind.

"I was just thinking about all the characters there at the restaurant. The girls who would have devoured you if you let them. The silver-haired couples. The wait staff, and the kitchen help."

"You should see it when I go overseas. Talk about a clash of cultures. Imagine if they were all speaking different languages."

She threw out a question she'd often thought about since high school. "Can you imagine if you wanted to orchestrate all these people coming together like they did tonight? If that was your job to choreograph that scene, how would you do it? When you think of it, it's a statistical miracle."

"Whoa! That's way beyond my bandwidth. You came up with that on your own?"

Aimee readjusted herself and smiled, facing front once again. "I could lie, and you'd think I was a genius. But I had a statistics professor in college who loved to throw that out to all his Freshmen. He said it was his proof that we were living in miracles every day."

"Or a grumpy farm boy like me might say it's proof of the randomness of life."

She couldn't suppress another smile. "Or you could say that."

"But man, what a place, right? Great food. Packed on a Wednesday night. That place is a goldmine."

Aimee was grateful for the conversation. "That's for sure."

"Except for the Flamingo Special. That one didn't grow on me like I thought it would."

"And I loved it," Aimee grinned. "They are so consistent, Andy. I never get tired of their jambalaya. Can you just imagine how much seafood they go through every evening?"

"And it was all fresh," he said. "I can see why you guys go back there so often."

"Creatures of habit."

"Purveyors of good taste," he corrected her.

She decided to let the differences stand where they fell and to change the subject.

"I guess we're going to be attending that wedding, then. I'm going to have to check my wardrobe because I don't think I have anything suitable to wear," she sighed.

"Well, after Cory told us about his little experience there, I don't think it's going to matter. We may only be in attendance for about five minutes, right?

Aimee nodded. "That was a new story for me. He must have thousands of them."

"He's got lots of stories all right. Some of them are even true."

She directed him to turn just after the dog park and the Pelican sanctuary. Although her house was a more expensive rental, though it was smaller than Cory's, she liked the neighborhood better.

"How long are you here for, or do you know?" he asked her.

"I'm on a two-month lease, but I can extend it up to a year if I want. Technically, it's just a month-to-month tenancy now."

"How come you don't move in with Cory? And don't answer that if it's too personal."

She leaned back into the comfortable lumbar support of the leather seat and smiled. "That's a good question, Andy. We've talked about it every once in a while, but it's sort of like I don't want to give up my house and he doesn't want to give up his. I couldn't tell you which one of us is the more stubborn, although he'll claim it's me."

"I can see the difference in the neighborhood already. Looks like they've torn down and rebuilt most of the smaller homes in this area. I think it's safer for a woman, living alone."

"And I have a handgun."

"Good to know," he said, nodding. "Bad for the bad guys."

"It belonged to my dad."

"You trained in how to use it, clean it, know the rules of engagement?"

"Not quite."

"You don't want to own a gun unless you're prepared to use it, Aimee. It will be far safer for you that way and for any innocent who happens to come across it. You should take it seriously."

She kept quiet. Finally, he added, "I don't mean to interfere, but you have to respect guns. Then it becomes a protective device and not something that could get you or someone else killed."

She didn't respond again.

"So I did it, didn't I?"

"You did. But I understand it was for my benefit. I'll add it to my list."

He touched her shoulder. "Thanks. Lecture over." Then he asked, "How did you find the place?"

"I couldn't believe I found it online. And it's quieter, too, than just about any other place I've looked at. The land slopes to the shore here, which makes it not quite as good for swimming, but it does block the traffic noise from Gulf Boulevard, and that's a huge plus." She pointed to the little bungalow on the beach. "Home sweet home."

Andy stopped the car and turned off the ignition. He accompanied her to her front door where she lingered.

"Are you going to be okay with Cory?"

"Just like I did the night before. He's a sack of potatoes."

She wanted to touch him but didn't want to be inappropriate. Taking the safe road, she extended her hand and they shook.

"It was fun. It was really, really fun, Andy. I can't remember when I've had such a day filled with so many activities. That morning run and breakfast was outstanding. Then we got the bikes. We ate ice cream and watched the sunset. Then danced at JJ's. It feels like a week has gone by. Normally, my life's a lot slower."

"Mine's a little different pace than that. When we're home, it's slow. But at work, things come up all the time. And you never know when it will just explode."

"Well, thank you, Andy. Now, do you want me to call Shelley and invite her for Saturday? Or do you want to do it?"

"Let me think about that for a little bit. Cory and I will talk it over unless you feel strongly about it."

"I just want to do whatever is more comfortable for you. I wonder if we should take two cars. That way, if someone wants to come home early, they can."

"Good point."

She suddenly realized that she was just making nervous conversation, like she didn't want him to leave. She gently placed that thought in the back of her mind, smiled, and said good night one more time.

Her house was a sanctuary of all the things she loved about living on the beach. She knew she was going to have to pay extra because she'd put so many holes in the wall with her must-have finds, mostly beach-themed plaques and pictures. A long turquoise fishing net stretched along one wall where she clipped favorite things to it with bright colored clothespins.

As was her nightly routine, she checked every window and every door to make sure they were locked. She had her father's handgun in the nightstand, loaded, but she doublechecked it anyway.

Andy would be proud.

The silvery water was calmer than it had been the night before.

She peeled off her clothes, took a quick hot shower, and snuggled into a flannel nightgown. It wasn't quite cool enough now to wear the nightgown, but it made her feel safe.

Lying on her back, she mentally set her internal alarm clock for six a.m., took a deep breath, and let it out slowly. As she sunk into sleep, she began to hear music from the dance floor and the sounds of those silly laughing wedding party ladies. She remembered the look of Andy's smile bathed in the magical sunset. She remembered the taste of her ice cream and the way the sun surrendered at last to the blue horizon.

Then she saw the face of the young man she thought looked like Logan. But sleep was beginning to overtake her, and she didn't have the energy to explore further.

CHAPTER 7

ON THE MORNING of the wedding, Cory got a phone call from Little Creek that he had to take in private.

Andy watched his buddy walk out onto the patio and plop down in one of his favorite yellow Adirondack chairs. He didn't want to spy on Cory, but it didn't look like a conversation that originated from SEAL Team 4.

Last night, he and Cory had begun to talk about Cory's drinking. His cast was coming off next week, and he said he was looking forward to driving again. The problem for Andy was he hadn't seen Cory without a beer in his hand just about anytime from late morning to bedtime.

It also was something he knew Aimee was concerned about. But since Andy hadn't been there a week yet, he decided to put off all the suggestions and confrontations until just before he left.

Cory had also received something in the mail from Little Creek, which he ripped into shreds and threw it out in the trash without showing it to anyone.

All these things had begun to add up. And while Andy wasn't worried about the significance of any of these by themselves, the combination was more than he was comfortable with.

He read the local flea market rag after he noticed Cory had glanced over his shoulder a couple of times to see if he was being observed. Andy made sure he kept his eyes on the paper.

Finally, the call ended, and Cory came back inside.

"Hey, Cory, you want to try one of my meal replacement shakes?" Andy asked.

"Sure thing. Where do you get it?"

"A couple of former team guys put together a company, and they did a lot of nutritional research too. We actually take some of their stuff on deployments now."

He pulled out two plastic bottles from his duffel bag, and showed Cory the powdery mixture filled to nearly a third. After adding water, he shook them both vigorously and then handed one to Cory.

"Keep shaking for a bit. They're all natural, but they don't always dissolve right away. You know how it goes. No pain, no gain."

"Gotcha."

Cory started dancing around the room, exaggerating the meal prep.

"All right, showoff. I think you have it now, Cory."

They shared a smile and then opened the shake. Andy was used to taking it down all at one time, but Cory taste tested it and wasn't quite sure at first if he liked it.

"It won't hurt you. Lots of kick ass vitamins and it helps you hydrate. Stores for years. It's good stuff"

"Is this something my system has to get used to?"

Andy shook his head. "I don't know what you mean exactly."

"Is it going to give me the shits?" Cory spelled out.

"Nope. Good and healthy. Nothing like that."

"Okay, down the hatch," he said and then belched.

Cory picked up the two empties, depositing them both in the garbage under the sink. He slowly wandered back and collapsed in the loveseat in front of him.

"So I have some news, and I need to let you in on a few things that I'm kind of working on."

Andy was relieved that finally he might be getting some answers. "That mean this phone call was good news?"

"Good and bad." He stared at the ceiling for a minute and then lowered his eyes, as he scrunched back into the seat. "Depending on what they find with my arm, and I'm pretty sure I'm going to be okay, I might be called up for an assignment."

The surprised Andy. "Where?"

"First, let me lay some groundwork. That trip to the sandbox was all screwed up, Andy. It was a huge botched job. People died who shouldn't have. And, I'll be honest with you, and I never want it to leave this room, some of that falls on me."

Andy knew this was serious. He adjusted his body and then leaned forward, resting his forearms on his knees. "You know, Cory, you shouldn't really blame yourself. Nothing ever works out exactly the way it's supposed to. Military stuff is messy even when the planning is nearly flawless. Stuff just happens."

"No shit. But I at least want to be honest with you. I mean we go over there as newbies, right? We try to follow the rules and follow instructions. But the bottom line is, even on the teams, you know we talk brotherhood and Rah Rah, everybody's together, and all that stuff. But if something goes wrong and the people in Washington or Norfolk start to look for answers or look for fault or blame, it's probably not gonna be the twenty-five-year guys they're going to blame."

"Yup. That's why we need to get a good LPO. My guy is great. I mean all of the guys on our platoon would die for this guy. And I've heard stories about all the people he saved, both civilian and military."

"I'm happy for you, Andy. But not all of them are like that. For some reason we had a whole cluster of newbies right out of the Academy. Anyway, I don't wanna make this too complicated, but the bottom line is there are a few people riding my ass. And it makes it even more important that I get this arm healed. But if I get injured again, they're probably going to quit me."

"For cause?"

"Not really, in my opinion. But you know shit rolls downhill, right?"

"Ha ha. And so that was your phone call?"

Cory burst out laughing. "Well, part of that was a little recreational thing."

"What does *that* mean?"

"I got a guy who sells me a little bit of weed now and then, to help me sleep. I found him through this girl that I met in the hospital actually. She's a nurse. I was trying to score something so I could go to sleep naturally. Weed does that for me. I'm still healing. I still have pain, and I have to get up. If I can't sleep well, I can't heal."

Andy couldn't believe what he was hearing. Cory had justified so many things, and he wondered if he still knew the difference between right and wrong. He thought about the expression 'dying of a thousand cuts,' and he wondered if the Navy had recommended he get some counseling.

"You should get a referral to somebody, Cory. I appreciate you telling me about all this stuff. But you need to talk to somebody else. It isn't healthy to not be sleeping, and as a matter of fact, you've been sleeping a lot, I think. So I don't quite understand. But if you need something to take before you go to bed, you should get it from the Navy. Let them manage it. Don't try to do it yourself, because it's dangerous."

"Now listen to you. Dangerous. We're fuckin' dangerous. That's what we do best." He scowled and crossed his legs. "But I even thought about that. Therein lies the problem. I don't want to give them anything that would make them want to toss me."

"Cory, have you even thought about this all being in your head, I mean maybe they're not really thinking that way. And asking for help, doesn't that show good leadership and courage? I'd hate to see you not get help just because you think it wouldn't look good on your file."

"Andy do you even watch the news? They're jacking guys all over the place for bullshit infractions right and left. Suicide rates are up. I mean, it's a mess. And to make matters worse, we're fighting a fucking war that we can't win."

"But that's not what we do, Cory. That's not our job. We're not supposed to ask those questions."

"Okay, Superman, I see where you're going with

this."

"So let's just say you had a really crappy deployment and especially badly planned operation. Next one will be better." Andy could see he wasn't buying it.

"Oh, I get you. Power of positive thinking and all. Get me some Yoga tapes and start doing meditation."

"Cory, you're just an angry asshole. I'm talking about taking some definitive, positive steps to first find out if they really are looking for an excuse to get rid of you, and second, trust the system to give you sound medical advice. Quit managing it on your own based on what you imagine is happening. In fact, I'm wondering if that's really you or the drugs working."

"We're just going to have to disagree on that. Give me a chance to share some things with you. But dammit, you gotta shut up and let me talk."

Andy knew he'd make a lousy counselor, and Cory had just confirmed it. "I apologize. Tell me your plan."

"Before I left Little Creek to come down here, I put in for an extra training round at the burn center in San Antonio at the joint base. They told me it was a long-shot, but since we had the long medical course, they said I might go to the top of the line. So I'm waiting for a slot."

Andy was thrilled.

"That's a good idea. Give yourself time to settle down. Heal up and in the meantime, get more training.

Man, why didn't you tell me that in the first place? I wouldn't have given you the lecture."

"No, that's my fault. So at first they told me they wouldn't consider the spot until I was clear, which made no sense whatsoever. I don't have to just sit around the beach doing nothing until my fucking arm heals. As much as I love it here, you and I, we're men of action. Anyway, I got a call yesterday, and they told me that there would be a place for me."

"When would you go there?"

"They said it could be in a couple of weeks or another month. But one way or the other, I'm going."

Andy was puzzled by all of the little parts of Cory's story that somehow just didn't smell right. "So what's the problem then, man?"

"First, there's Aimee. And to be fair, she hasn't made any claim on me, Andy. She's been great. I'm a better man because of her. But I feel bad just getting up and leaving her, because I never told her about the letter or what I had applied for. I knew in the back of my head that this might happen, and I didn't tell her."

Andy was glad Cory was considerate of Aimee's feelings. "That's a good thing, Cory. If you love each other, you being gone for a few months isn't going to mess that up."

"Well, I was thinking I could ask her to marry me, and she could go with me to San Antonio."

Andy stared in disbelief. This wasn't at all what he was expecting to hear.

After several seconds of silence, Cory ventured a comment. "So I guess you don't think it's a good idea?" Cory jumped to his feet and started nervously pacing back-and-forth.

Andy wasn't sure what he should tell him. "I'm just shocked is all. Hey, if that's what you wanna do, go for it, go for all of it."

Cory drilled him a look but nearly seared his eyeballs. "I want to know what you're thinking, Andy. I want your *opinion*."

"I don't have an opinion. It's not one of those things that has anything to do with me. It's something you and Aimee should work out. Like I said before, whether she stays here, or she goes with you to San Antonio, those are all things you need to sit down and talk about. It doesn't matter one wit what I think. You gotta do what's right for you. And if this is the next step for you two, then I say go for it."

"That's what I thought you'd say. And I want to thank you for being honest. I got some details to work out, and of course, I don't have a spot until I see the paperwork, damn paperwork. But I know that with Aimee, it would be the kind of support I need to get through that course, and then she could help me decide where I'm going with the teams."

"Just. Be. Honest. That's my advice from start to finish, Cory. That also means taking a look at what we talked about earlier, getting some help, not doing the illicit stuff, cleaning your act up. She's a great gal. Very rare person, and I agree. I think she'd really be good for you."

Cory walked over to the picture window, placed his forearm against the glass, rested his forehead on the cast, and mumbled, "And I think I'd be really good for her too."

Andy hadn't seen any of this coming. Something made him nervous. He suddenly discovered what it was.

He felt an overwhelming need to protect her. That was beginning to be a problem.

How in the world can I be a best friend to my buddy when I know the woman he says he loves would be better off without him?

CHAPTER 8

AIMEE SPENT THE better part of the morning looking for one perfect dress. The ceremony was to take place at the Presbyterian Church in Sarasota, the old First Church, starting at four.

The plan was to attend the reception afterwards. She offered to drive so she could keep the boys, primarily Cory, out of trouble. Cory insisted they attend both. Because she'd never been to a huge formal society wedding before, she was glad she could be the only woman at the party with two dates.

Poetic justice.

The boys were to pick her up at her place around three.

She got up early, skipping a run, and got an appointment to have her hair cut and highlights added at a shop nearby. She also had an appointment to get her nails and toes done. At ten o'clock, when the mall opened, she planned to hit Neiman Marcus as well as a specialty high end bridal and formal shop nearby.

As far as jewelry, she had one set of pearls, which belonged to her mother. And that was going to have to do. She just needed to buy a dress with a scoop neckline, which would really showcase the beautiful pearls. Her father had spent nearly two months' salary to buy them for her, or so the story went. Her mother had cherished them and worn them all the time. Every time they went to the symphony in Davis, or she was invited to lunch somewhere, or they went to San Francisco for a play or opera or ballet, her mother wore the pearls. This would be the first time Aimee would wear them.

The Brides and Belle's shop was first on her list, since she'd read online it was where several of the society ladies had shopped in the past. It was just one dress and one pair of matching shoes she was investing in, so she felt like she could splurge.

No one knew that she had the proceeds of her parents' Tennessee home already in the bank, and she planned on keeping it that way as long as she could. When she was good and ready, she'd start looking to buy a little house like she was renting. But she wasn't ready just yet. She considered purchasing something she could later tear down and build something larger, but still modest. Right on the beach. That's where she knew she wanted to be. She could afford to be picky and take her time.

But for right now, the 1200 square-foot cottage suited her just fine.

She checked her watch and calculated she'd have about four hours to complete her shopping, and then she had to allow an hour to get home. She set her alarm for two o'clock, which would give her enough time to shower again and be ready for the boys to pick her up at three.

Just in case she couldn't find anything, Plan B was to wear the short sleeve cocktail dress with the pearls, even though it was black. But that was Plan B. She was going for something a little more exciting.

Once she walked through the front door, an attractive woman in her fifties introduced herself and asked her if she'd like a cappuccino. She was led to a small and very private sitting area with mirrors on three sides. It was furnished in red flowered wallpaper, which matched the red leather couch and ottoman. This "little" waiting room, as her helper described it, was larger than her dorm room at UC Davis.

Marlene brought her cappuccino in on a silver tray. "I slipped a couple biscuits in for you, since shopping sometimes causes us to miss lunch. I hope that was all right."

THE WOMAN SAT on the ottoman, crossed her legs, and placed a clipboard on her thigh, her pen poised, ready to take notes.

"So you said this is a big wedding? A society wedding?"

"Yes."

"Okay, and how much time do we have to get the dress ready?"

"The wedding's this afternoon."

Marlene looked like she'd just seen a naked man walk into the office. She quickly recovered, slid back onto the ottoman, and crossed her legs the other direction.

"Most of these dresses in the store are samples, which is what we order from. Many of them are just pinned so we can fit you perfectly. I can perhaps call and see if I can locate a certain dress if you find one here that you like. We also have some sale dresses. So I don't want to get your hopes up, dear. I'm not sure we'll be able to accommodate you today."

Aimee considered what she'd been told. "So then show me the dresses that you have in stock, if you have any. Once I see my choices, I can make a decision quite easily."

"What's your budget?"

She'd not thought about that. "If I like it, I'll buy it. I don't have a budget. I want something that will make me look fabulous. I want to blow my boyfriend's mind and make every other single girl at the party jealous."

Aimee grinned.

"Color?"

"Something bright and dazzling. No white or off-white of course. That's reserved for the bride. Is that correct?"

"Indeed." Marlene made some notes on her clipboard, asked questions about her normal dress size, picked up a telephone, and requested the in-house seamstress join the two of them. "She will take exact measurements, so we can see if perhaps we can find a top that fits you perfectly. The skirt can be a different size if you need to. We have lots of flexibility that way."

Aimee thought that was a clever way to approach the problem.

"So what color is it that, when people see you wearing it, they tell you that you're stunning. Most people have one color that they just absolutely love wearing. What color is that for you, Aimee?"

"It would have to be red."

"Red, as in blood red, orange red, pinkish red?"

"Fire engine red. Five-alarm red. Bright, no gray tones."

"Is the wedding in a church or outdoors at a venue?"

"The wedding is at the old First Church in Sarasota. The reception is at the Sarasota country club. It's called something else, but apparently, it's a big beautiful one."

"That would probably be the Sarasota Silverado?"

"That's it. The Silverado."

"So can I ask you who the bride and groom are?"

"The groom's name, I think, is Moore, and I was told the family breeds horses. Racehorses?"

"I know exactly who will be at that wedding." She tilted her head and asked, "This will be quite an event. Are you friends of the bride or groom?"

"Bride. My boyfriend and I recently met her at JJs near St Pete Beach."

"Well, you're a very lucky lady. Don't be surprised if you wind up dancing with Tiger Woods or a famous NFL or baseball player. The Moores also own a hockey team, as well as two Mexican league professional soccer teams. They're lovely people."

Marlene checked her watch and frowned. Picking up the phone again, she demanded to know why the seamstress had not checked in with her. While she was on hold, there was a gentle knock on the door.

Aimee opened it and looked down at an elderly seamstress, wearing a black apron with multiple pockets in the front. She wore three plastic tape measures strung around her neck like a stethoscope. She carried a small pad of paper and a pencil.

The woman spoke to Marlene in a Latino dialect. They exchanged information, and after, the diminutive lady nodded her head. She walked around Aimee, making notes, and then located a square stool that was hiding in the corner and placed it in the middle of the room. She motioned for Aimee to step up on it.

The seamstress's gnarled fingers suffered from arthritis, with her third and fourth fingers on her right hand the most advanced. She slipped one of the tape measures off her neck and began making calculations, jotting down various lengths. Her quiet, deliberate movements made quick work of everything, and she was done in less than ten minutes.

Tucking the pencil behind her ear, the woman explained her findings to Marlene. She gave a sweet smile to Aimee and then let herself out.

"Come, come. Finish your cappuccino, and then let's go see some dresses, shall we?"

As Marlene walked down the narrow space between overstuffed rows of beautiful gowns from sherbets to more vibrant colors, her fingers traced over the clear plastic zipper bags. Aimee soon realized that it could easily take her days to look at every beautiful dress.

"How in the world am I to decide?" Aimee asked.

"First, look at color. That's the easiest decision. And then we have to decide whether you want a floor-length gown or mid-calf or knee."

"You don't categorize them by style?"

Marlene had a huge laugh at that suggestion. "Every gown is different, and because of all the beading and intricate decorative work, that would be impossible. So let me show you what we have in red. That's a good place to start."

They carefully passed through a forest of light pink and yellow dresses, having to turn sideways to navigate the narrow channel. The majority of these were wedding gowns, but as they turned the corner, Aimee was ushered into a large classroom sized-space that was lined with racks of red cocktail dresses and gowns of varying lengths. In the center were several project tables, littered with plastic trays containing sequins, pearls, and ribbon. One woman was stitching pearls and rhinestones onto the white bodice top to a wedding dress.

Aimee turned her attention to the stuffed rows of gowns, pulling out ones that were the true red color she had in mind. Marlene examined her choices, and began relocating similarly colored dresses to a portable clothes rack so she could try them on.

In the space of an hour, Aimee found a dress exactly like what she pictured in her mind. As she stood on a pedestal in front of an arc of mirrors, the seamstress came back in and pinned the length for her. Within minutes, the hem was cut and the skirt on its way to being finished off. The seamstress made a note to adjust the waist by taking the fabric in nearly an inch.

Marlene handed her a strip of fabric that had been removed from the gown, and motioned for her to come up to the front of the store.

"What's this for?" Aimee asked.

"I'm going to have you pay for the dress now, and you can take that fabric to help you find your shoes. Your dress will be finished by the time you come back. If you can't find the right color, then buy something in bone or white. We can dye them to match, so keep that in mind if you find a comfortable pair you like."

"But I was thinking of some fancy sandals with heels, this being Florida. Something with rhinestones."

"Yes, you could do that. Make sure anything you buy has a one or two inch heel. Not only is that what your hem is measured for, it's easier to dance with a low heel than with a flat or a high heel. Just pick what you like and, remember, don't buy something too small or you'll have to sit out most of the dancing."

Aimee paid more for the gown than she'd ever paid for a dress before. But she was going to turn this into a Cinderella ball and hoped to capture the attention of her Prince Charming.

She located a comfortable pair of jeweled sandals that showed off her newly polished red toes, returned to the bridal shop, and tried the dress on one more time with sandals. Everything was perfect.

Marlene helped her load the dress into her car, gave her a chaste hug, and thanked her for her business. The entire shopping spree, including purchasing a new special bra, had taken her less than two hours. She was on her way back to Sunset Beach and had time to spare.

AIMEE WAS GLAD the men arrived early. She waited until she saw Andy's car before she put her dress on. Her nerves were firing on all rockets. She'd had to dab a towel to her underarms a dozen times in the last hour.

She examined herself in the bathroom mirror and approved. The bright red dress had a low-cut, form-fitting bodice that had necessitated her new undergarment, making her chest look twice her normal size. A multi-layered puffy sleeve draped at one shoulder, sloping down and off her other shoulder to leave it bare. The pearls were the perfect, simple complement to the elegant lines.

The skirt was slightly gathered. Layers of the lush red fabric pulled to the sides over her hips and attached at the back of her waistband in a faux bustle. She twirled, feeling the weight of the fabric perfect for the dance floor. It showed off all her best features and swayed with her body's movement. She had never felt more beautiful.

Aimee was glad her hairdresser convinced her to wear her hair down, showing off the new vanilla streaks and highlights she'd gotten this morning. She used more than her usual share of blush then added the bright lipstick and gloss. Since she was not used to seeing herself in makeup, the woman in the mirror almost looked like a strange guardian angel from one of her dreams.

Butterflies were not just fluttering inside her stomach, they were growling like bees, as she walked through her tiny living room and opened the door.

She'd never seen either of the SEALs in suits and ties, so the handsome gentlemen who were going to escort her to the wedding and party looked totally foreign. She could see they were having the same reaction to her. Nobody spoke. Cory's jaw was still gaping, his eyes wide.

Andy punched him in the arm so he closed his mouth and leaned forward to give Aimee a kiss.

She broke the ice. "Wow. Just wow. You guys are going to steal the show. Did you have to buy new suits?"

Cory nodded, rocking on his brand new black leather lace-ups.

"Shoes too?" she asked.

"Which are going to come off as soon as we can get away with it," muttered Andy. "I've already got a small blister just walking to and from the car." He fidgeted and then added, "But look at you, Aimee. I'm stunned. You're going to eclipse the bride! Don't you think, Cory?"

Cory was leaning against the doorway, his palm to his forehead, overcome. "You outdid yourself. We're going to be busy all night fighting off all the other guys, maybe even the groom, who I hear is a billionaire, so no games, okay?"

"Thank you." She could feel her cheeks heating up. "I'm totally speechless, at how handsome you two are." Aimee gasped.

"Ready?" Cory presented his elbow.

"Let me get my scarf." Aimee brought along an oversized red and white silk scarf her parents had brought to her from Hong Kong. With the bare shoulder, she wanted to be able to stay warm. If there was any wind, she'd need the cover.

They escorted her to the passenger side of the Jeep. Her skirt was a little restrictive getting in, even with the running bar, so Cory picked her up by the waist and hoisted her into the seat. Andy rounded the front and climbed into the driver's side.

She grabbed Cory's hand. "Where's your cast?"

"It didn't fit, so I cut it off."

"Cory!"

"I'm fine. It's only three days early. No biggie."

Andy was muttering in the driver seat, rolling his eyes. She started to ask him if he helped.

"Don't," he said, holding his palm up. "I caught him using a drill trying to get the thing off. He was lucky I walked in on him, or I think we'd all be waiting in the Emergency Room." And then he added, "And he'd still try to operate on himself if he could."

Aimee had told Andy she was more independent and stubborn than Cory, but now realized she'd been wrong.

The drive was easy and the traffic light. They parked, and then she hooked her arm in Cory's, and all three of them approached the church.

Several reporters were outside taking pictures of celebrities, and it wasn't long before they noticed the trio.

"Here comes our red carpet moment," Andy whispered.

Cory leaned in from the other side of Aimee, adding, "They'll never believe this in Coronado, will they?"

"I'm going to catch all kinds of hell for it," Andy shot back, whispering between his teeth, trying to give a winning smile to the photographer.

Aimee linked arms with Andy as well. "When the girls find you, it's going to be an Elvis moment, but I'm going to claim both of you, just so we're clear."

"I'm pulling for a cake fight over you, Andy. Hell,

the bride might change her mind and grab you." Cory was just warming up with the jabs and pranks.

"In your dreams, Drillmaster. She'd take one look at my bank account and ask me if it was my beer money."

"It is. That's where it went," Cory answered as he turned and posed for a photo op. "Who cares if you're rich if you can't use your noodles."

Aimee gasped.

They paused to allow several long white limos to cross their path and park.

"See what you did?" whispered Andy. "On second thought, keep it up, ToolTime. Then I'll have the lady all to myself."

"Stop!" Aimee demanded. "You're making me crazy, and it's embarrassing. Can we just go inside and behave?"

Neither man said a word, but within seconds, they were both nearly doubling over in laughter.

"So much for manners. This is the bride's special day. Let's not ruin it," she scolded.

Cory leaned forward and whispered back, "I think Andy could make it even more special, right, Casanova? Or did you buy a crystal candy dish instead?"

Aimee dropped her arms and stormed off in front of them. She knew the comments they made about how the bustle on her backside bounced seductively were spoken just loud enough so she'd hear them.

She turned around briefly and glared at them.

The two SEALs stopped in their tracks. "You're right. She's even prettier when she's mad," said Andy.

Aimee whipped around and arrived at the church's foyer several seconds before they did. She was preparing to be escorted to the left side, but Cory intervened.

"No, no, no. Ain't happening, sport," he said as he removed Aimee's arm from the usher's clutches and unceremoniously pushed him aside.

The young usher's face turned bright red as he searched the church for an ally. Cory took off with Aimee in tow, searching for a seat.

Andy leaned over and whispered to the boy, "Better leave him be. He's a natural-born killer. An elite Navy SEAL. He wears ear necklaces and eats raw meat. I'd recommend not messing with him."

Cory started making dead cat noises, having difficulty holding in a laughing meltdown. Aimee could only imagine the expression that must have been on the young usher's face. At last, they found seats, Aimee between the two SEALs.

"Behave!" she whispered.

"Yes, ma'am." Cory said.

Andy didn't answer.

The smell of fresh flowers was intoxicating, and before long, Aimee noticed several members of the audience had begun to sneeze and cough. And then it hit Cory, who sneezed in a honk, like there was a horn lodged in his throat. People turned their heads.

"Now I know how you got kicked out." she murmured. "Can't you do *anything* without drawing attention?"

"Probably not, sweetheart. But at least I'm yours." He kissed the side of her cheek in an uncharacteristically sweet gesture.

It was a long, elegant ceremony. When they exited the church, the sky was turning bright orange, which meant there would be a gorgeous sunset at the beach. They followed the long line of cars, winding through neighborhoods with world-class tropical gardens and mansions nestled in the foliage large enough to look like hotels. Elegant gates guarded everything.

At the country club security gate, Andy handed in their invitation so they could be admitted. They parked under the shade of a cluster of palms.

They were ushered into a complex of enormous connecting white tents sporting brightly-colored flags. They were asked to sign the guest register, and Aimee did so, then handed the pen to Andy. Cassanova and ToolTime added theirs right below.

Bouquets of flowers, mostly shades of peach pastels and ivory roses, were hanging upside down so that people traveling under them would be showered with a heady aroma. Embedded in the flowers were LED lights that twinkled. It was truly a stunning display.

Cory immediately steered her to the bar like it was a grave emergency. Andy followed not far behind but got held up by the ladies of the bride's wedding party.

"You came!" Ginger said as she gave him a bear hug he wasn't ready for.

"Let's get him a drink," Cory whispered.

Aimee watched the ladies engage Andy in conversation. He looked smashing in his black suit. They peppered him with questions and were clearly vying for his attention. He was patient, taking the time to speak to each of them, even though she noticed he held his hands together and appeared a bit stiff. He caught her glance and smiled back, arching his eyebrows, to tell her he was uncomfortable with all the attention. Aimee had known men half as good-looking who were way more wrapped up in themselves.

Casanova. It was the perfect description.

"Come on, Hot Lips, let's rescue the old guy," Cory said as he handed her a glass of champagne. He held two long-necked beers in his other. Aimee followed. She noticed the relief in Andy's eyes at the sight of Cory coming to his aid. Cory jumped right in the middle of the circle to take some of the pressure off Andy. But Aimee realized, unlike Andy, Cory was completely comfortable and in his element.

She stood outside the ring of ladies surrounding the two SEALs, alone, enjoying the dance of mating rituals as old as the world.

CHAPTER 9

Andy watched Cory and Aimee on the dance floor. Of all the things he did for her, he was most appreciative of the fact that Cory made her laugh. He just made her happy.

Sometime during the weekend, Cory was going to let Aimee know about his plans to move to Texas. The burden felt heavy on Andy's soul, as if he was not keeping a promise. But he pushed it away, knowing that he sometimes had a penchant for overthinking and worrying about too many things.

When he looked at the staging of this affair—from the decorations to the money spent on throwing such a lavish party—it occurred to him that the bride's family was more interested in making a statement than celebrating the marriage of their daughter. Something about the whole scene was a little off, out of control, like a grandiose corporate event that must have cost a fortune and taken months in the planning. Another message, something else could have been done instead. Something personal.

Aimee danced with numerous other guests, while Cory talked to a table of people, telling stories or overtipping the bartender to make stronger drinks. Cory acted like it was his party, given in his honor. He talked too much about what they did as an elite unit. The alcohol made him boastful and proud, looking for praise that he never could get enough of.

Someone had to watch over *Aimee* in Cory's absence. Someone had to make sure that where they placed their hands on her body was appropriate, giving her the respect she so deserved.

One particular slow dance had him nearly jump to his feet and tear her out of the older man's clutches. The guy's palm wandered from her waist and down along her backside, which made Aimee jump.

But Andy waited, held himself back, because as they turned, he saw Aimee was smiling. He began to understand that she'd probably smile through everything in life. She was all alone, but she wasn't lonely. He knew that Cory was a flawed individual, but Aimee would always see the good in him. No matter what.

Several women had made advances toward him, letting him know that he could ask them to dance. He even offered a couple of times. He chatted with people who passed him as he stood against the wall and watched the arena like he used to evaluate battle scenes.

He remembered the lines of girls in high school who stood together talking all evening, trying to look like they were perfectly fine with being a wallflower. Some of them would stand there all night long and never be asked to dance. They'd probably go home and share it with their pillow. He could never do that. He wondered why they tried.

Maybe that's the difference between men and women. Maybe they try harder.

In Aimee's case, she was kind and did it because it was the right thing to do. And *because* it was the right thing to do, it made her feel happy.

But things changed as Andy sipped on his third beer. He took the blinders off his heart. That's when he realized something was growing there. And it went far beyond just wanting to protect another person. In a very short period of time, she had become more than just a sister, more than just his best friend's girl.

He wasn't going to go there this evening. That would be something he could consider when he was all alone, watching the waves or lying in his bed at night wondering, about…

Aimee caught him watching her. She murmured something to her partner and sauntered through various tables. Her head tilted to the side, not showing any embarrassment and not asking permission before wrapping herself in his gaze. He could see she'd figured it out. She knew he thought she was the most beautiful woman in the whole world. In her confidence and grace as she approached him she was telling him that she knew all those things, and more.

This is so dangerous.

"Do I have to ask you to dance, Andy?" she said when she reached him.

He stumbled with his answer when she took his hand and pulled him off the wall and toward the dance floor. He didn't want it to look like he was being dragged so he walked alongside her.

"I must've danced with ten different men tonight, but you never asked me once. Why is that?" she asked, her eyes focused on her trajectory.

"I-I was going to. Just didn't want to get in the way." The frog in his throat was extremely unfortunate.

Still holding his hand, she stood still, studying his face as if looking for something in his eyes. Luckily for Andy, he was an expert at masking what he didn't want others to see.

"Then I guess I have to ask *you*. Dance with me, Andy."

Her breath and her desire washed over him, making the request deeper than her words.

"I'd love to. I've wanted to all night long." It was

just loud enough for only her ears.

She turned again, and he followed behind her just as the last song was ending.

"I have to warn you, Aimee, I'm not a very good dancer."

She turned. "Nonsense. I've been watching."

As they approached the dance floor, he searched the room for Cory and found him having an intense conversation with Ginger, the redheaded bridesmaid. For a fleeting second, Andy wished Cory would show up to rescue him from what he knew was going to be a very dangerous and indulgent few minutes.

He glanced in the corner again and saw Cory kiss the girl, and he was so disappointed. He hoped Aimee didn't see the transgression so boldly played.

And then a whole new set of emotions and feelings rose as he felt her step into his space, and lay a palm in the middle of his back, while he took Aimee in his arms for the slow dance that had just started.

It was one thing to sit with her on the beach, talk to her over the campfire, go for a morning run, or share a crab omelet. It was quite another to feel her body moving under his touch, responding to him, as he remained careful, respectful and she ever so slightly held him closer and tighter against him.

He could feel her breath against his chest and noticed a pleasant heat from her body warmed him all the way to his soul every place he touched her. She smelled like heaven itself. Her red lips matched the fabric of her flowing dress that enhanced her tiny waist. That whatever-you-call-it-thing on her butt was a challenge, telegraphing her stubbornness, her backbone for good, and her strength of character.

He was lacking that strength right now, stepping too close to the edge but unable to stop.

He looked down on the top of her head. It would've been so easy to just take a few strands of her hair that fell at the top on her shoulder and slip it behind her ear. He might let his finger trace over her neck and up to her lips just to see if she'd run away. He wanted to know, if he touched her there, would she shrink back?

It was so wrong to think about this. And it was also equally wrong to know full well that if he had to hurt someone, he would probably have to hurt her. Because it was absolutely unthinkable to fall for a SEAL brother's lady. That promise had been made long before he met Aimee.

But there was no question he was falling, perhaps to the point of not being trusted.

For right now, he danced with her. He let his thumb make a slight movement back and forth on her back between her shoulder blades. He could enjoy and accept her delicate warmth, as she inched closer still and arched her back in response. He answered her subtle response by pressing her tighter against him, feeling her heavy breathing and sinking in deeper, entwining and entangling themselves further.

She looked up at him and licked her lips, her eyes focused on him. The music stopped but he was hesitant to let her go, and she didn't try to leave. He knew she wasn't afraid to show him something that she could not say. Something that had to remain a secret.

He was risking too much, and the pain of knowing it was her risk as well made it all the more tragic. There was honor in that gaze she gave him. If he crossed that line, that honor would be lost.

He looked for Cory again and was unsuccessful. One of the bridesmaids descended upon them.

"Can I steal this hunk of a man?"

Once again, it pleased Aimee to see him desired. "I warn you, he'll sweep you off your feet, pull your heart out, and return it bloody," she said with a little laugh.

Now Andy's embarrassment started to bloom. The bridesmaid moved her hips from side to side, closed her eyes and pulled her hair on top of her head as she conjured her best feminine spirits. But of course, her potion was powerless against him. He pretended to answer her movements and give her a little of what she was expecting. But when he closed his eyes, his arms were around Aimee's naked waist as she shattered beneath him.

Oh God, I've descended into Hell.

Mercifully, the dance was over. He searched for their table but found no trace of either Aimee or Cory.

"Another?" she asked him. Her upper lip was moist with tiny beads of sweat.

"I'll take a raincheck. Gotta go check on something."

He worried, as he traveled outside into the gardens surrounding the tent city, that if Cory was doing something he shouldn't and Aimee might stumble upon him. He tore back inside, checking the dark corner he'd seen Cory in before and found it empty. He checked the bar near the wedding cake set up where a crowd had gathered to watch the bride and groom cut the five-tiered cake tastelessly decorated with horses.

Beyond the crowd, he spotted Aimee coming from the restroom, and he sighed in relief. She slipped by the gathering and returned to their table to join him. As she slid her chair up to the table, her leg brushed against his.

He placed his hand over hers and whispered, "I can't. I want to, but I can't. And I won't lie."

She focused on their hands lying flat against each other. She turned her palm up and then wove her fingers through his and squeezed before pulling away.

It felt like a kiss.

He didn't have to tell her she and Cory needed to

talk. It would be wrong of him to let her know of his suspicions about her boyfriend, because that didn't have anything to do with how he felt for Aimee. Someone would think it was a crime of passion, and opportunity, yet it was so painful not to be able to explain all this to her. She turned her back to him and watched the dancers, showing him the perfect, soft skin he was hungry to explore.

Pretty girls were misbehaving on the dance floor, much to the delight of everyone who knew what it was like to be young, overflowing with passion and utterly dangerous. Andy continued to look for Cory.

He whispered in her ear. "Do you know where Cory is? I haven't seen him in awhile."

She turned her head slowly, her eyes drunk with lust. "Did you mean what you said?"

He wondered if she hadn't heard him properly. "Cory. I was asking you if you'd seen Cory."

"I saw him with some of the groomsmen." She smiled. "I'm guessing he's over in the cigar and brandy tent."

That made sense, and he was relieved.

"I should go check on him. He's had a lot to drink."

"Yes, I'm noticing the pattern too," she said coldly.

Andy stood. "I'll be right back."

She took his hand again. "Did you mean it?" she asked again.

"Every word," he whispered as he bent and kissed her on the cheek.

He asked directions to the brandy and cigar tent and headed in that direction. Something on his right caught his eye. He saw a white gazebo off in the distance and, after examining further, thought he saw movement there.

He toyed with the idea he should take the high road and check the tent first, but he played his hunch and made an arc to the other side of the structure so he'd be out of the path of the entrance.

It didn't take long before he could hear the sounds of two people. And they weren't talking. Between the gasps and moans, he could hear Cory's unmistakable whispers and the word *sweetheart* he'd heard so many times over the past week.

A concrete bench stood nearby, and he collapsed on it and hung his head, his elbows resting on his knees. His eyes teared up while he waited for the confrontation he knew was brewing.

He felt like he was back in Africa, helpless to tackle the wide range of situations and events that he had to be ready for at a moment's notice. Everything would be fine. They'd get their work done. Their presence needed to protect a village during a health vaccination program, or to make sure a duly elected official suddenly voted out of office would indeed vacate. Wars were fought over little things or things that started out small, at least. Most of the time, their Team just waited like he was doing right now. And then, someone would do something stupid, or maybe just make an honest mistake or act on faulty intelligence.

His stay at Sunset Beach was supposed to be lazy, filled with fishing and lying out in the sun. Get reacquainted with his buddy. Except that he hadn't realized his buddy returned from the Middle East a different guy than Andy remembered him to be. And that really scared him.

If he'd known all that, he would have turned down Cory's offer. He could have just chilled in Coronado with some of his other friends. Except then he wouldn't have met Aimee.

And that put a dangerous spin on everything. For his own sanity, he should leave right now and avoid the confrontations coming up. Except that would make him dishonorable, and he couldn't have that.

Somewhere in the distance, a sprinkler was going off. The yellow glow coming from the tents, mixed with the sounds of music and laughter, belied the fact that all was *not* as well as it seemed.

He heard shuffling of feet and a woman's soft giggle. Someone, probably Cory, asked for silence. Something was whispered, and then Andy heard the sound of woman's heels scampering down the stairs.

He saw the redhead, pretty Ginger, with her skirts lifted, running across the lawn and disappearing inside the tent.

Andy stood, walking slowly to the base of the stairs, put his hands in his pants, and hung his head. He didn't want to do this.

"Shit, Andy. You scared the piss out of me!" said Cory.

"What the hell are you doing, man?"

"I don't understand," Cory answered, searching the grounds.

"She's back at the party. I think I'm the only one who knows. But of course you know, you asshole."

"Hey, wait a minute. Don't go all hero on me. It's not what you think"

"Really?" Andy hated the sight of him.

Cory climbed down the stairs and faced him. "Okay, it was a mistake. She's been after me all night. And this is something you *don't* know. Aimee… well, Aimee and I haven't fucked in about two weeks."

"What does that have to do with it? Do you think any of that could be your fault? You know, Cory, this and the whole story about you wanting to get married and shit, it's really gotten old. What happened to you, man? This is not the guy I knew."

Cory hung his head. "I know what you're thinking, and I want to make it right, Andy. I'm so sorry."

"You're apologizing to *me?*"

"Okay, okay, I got it. I fucked up. I think the pills, the booze, and the lack of affection has just messed with my head. I'll completely turn things around. You'll see."

"You're not listening to me, Cory. You're affecting everyone around you. Are you going to make me lie to Aimee? Do I have to do that for you? Do I have to watch you make nice to her, try to con her into your graces? You're lyin', man."

"It all happened after the deployment, Andy."

"Horse shit. Nobody gets out of here without making their share of mistakes. But, Cory, the thing is, you know you're making them and you keep doing it. You can't stop, can you?"

Cory brushed over blades of grass with his toe.

"You're right."

"You need to quit the pills, stop the alcohol, and go get counseling."

"Look, Andy, I'm stronger than that. Maybe, if you help me, we can do it together, brother. Would you help me?"

"Listen to yourself. It's embarrassing, Cory. I don't want to be any part of that, Cory. I don't want anyone thinking I condone that behavior. You need professional help. Maybe you need to go to a clinic. I think the Navy would pay for—"

"Shut up. I can't tell the Navy. They'll toss me."

"They *should* toss you. You could get yourself and someone else killed. You're spinning out of control. Making bad decisions. You're going to lose Aimee, you know."

"Not if she doesn't know."

"That's B.S. and you know it."

"Well, if you're not going to help, you butt out of my business. You get the fuck out of my house and get yourself back to San Diego. I want your word you won't meddle in my relationship. You know that's wrong."

Andy should have told him he'd already stepped over the line. It was a technical infraction, but it was just as if he and Aimee had slept together all the same. But Cory didn't deserve the truth, just like he didn't deserve Aimee.

One part of Cory's argument was sound. Andy was going to have to step away and let them work it out on their own. If Cory could really straighten up and be the man he once was, it wasn't his place to take that away from him, despite his feelings for Aimee. He doubted it could be done, but he had to give Cory the chance.

But if he broke her heart or harmed her in any way, Andy would have to insert himself, and get in his face, because she deserved protection. She deserved the truth. If she didn't get it from Cory, somehow, she'd get it from him.

He owed that to her.

"You go to Texas, Cory. You tell her about your pill problems and tell her you're going away partly to work on yourself. She'd probably wait for you, you lucky sonofabitch. But you gotta be honest with her." Andy delivered the ultimatum even though he was filled with doubt and more than a little sadness.

"Okay. And what about you?"

"This is in no way about me."

"But you won't say anything?'

"Not if you tell the truth, Cory. Not if you come clean. And you need to come clean about all of it—the girls—"

"Wait! That will end the relationship right there."

Andy's doubts just increased tenfold. He was in such a horrible situation. He was close to just blowing the whole thing up.

"Can you change, Cory?"

"With some help, yes, I think I can."

"Do you want to change? Even if it means you're tossed off the teams?"

Cory was looking for angles. Andy knew how his mind worked.

"It's a lot to take in. You're probably right. I need some help. I should give her a break, but on one condition."

"What's that?'

"You don't take my place. You let me handle it."

"You better come clean and get honest with her. No more B.S., Cory. I won't be a part of that. She deserves better. She deserves the truth. And it's your story to tell, not mine. So I'll stay out of it as long as you're working on getting honest and clean."

Andy wished that he'd not just promised this to Cory. He knew he would fail, but he had to give him the chance.

"Agreed. I'm turning over a new leaf, starting tonight." Cory held his arms out to the side. Andy gave him the embrace that was asked for.

"Good luck. I'll get a motel room for the night. I'll ride back with you guys so I can make sure you get home safe, and then I'm out of here."

"You're a good friend, Andy. A true brother."

"Yeah. Well, don't make me wish I didn't make that promise to you. I mean it, Cory. I'll be your worst nightmare."

CHAPTER 10

AIMEE KNEW IMMEDIATELY something was very wrong. Andy had been gone too long, but when she saw Cory step through the far tent opening with Andy close behind, they both of them quickly darted looks in her direction and then glanced away. She knew it was bad news.

The usual bevy of female attention surrounded Cory as he tried to make his way to her, but he seemed not to be interested. He pushed his way through the little crowd like a celebrity running from the media.

Many of the other guests were preparing to leave, and the reception took on the atmosphere of a changing of the guard. There were those who were nowhere near being partied out getting ready for some serious hell-raising. The other half appeared to be those who were ready to go home.

Just by the way Cory and Andy walked, she knew they were all three in the latter group. Neither man smiled. Neither man sought her attention from across the room. And when they got closer to the table, Cory averted his eyes. She sucked it up, hoping whatever had gone on outside in Andy's search wasn't too serious.

"There you are," she began. "I was beginning to think some of the bridesmaids had kidnapped you both. I'm glad I don't have to call the police." She played dumb and discovered they saw through the ruse.

Andy's expression was one of extreme internal pain. It was impossible to read him. Cory finally sat down and took her hand. She gulped in air and braced herself.

"Sweetheart, we have to leave. And…" He looked up at Andy first, and then blurted out the rest of his communication. "We need to talk."

"About what?" she demanded.

"Not here," he whispered, lowering his head so no one else could hear.

Her spine stiffened as she withdrew her hand, stood, picked up her purse, and threw the scarf around her shoulders. If Andy was going to shut her out and there was gonna be some kind of an argument or situation, she completely agreed with Cory. This was not the place she wanted it to happen. Clearly, her Cinderella evening was over.

"I'm going to go say goodbye to the bride and

groom," she muttered, staring down at Cory's seated frame.

"Fine. You go ahead, and we'll meet you in the car." Cory added a brittle smile, which made Aimee feel worse. Andy continued avoiding eye contact and had his hands stuffed in his pockets. Finally, his face blank, he nodded agreement with Cory's statement.

She found the bride and groom in a cluster of family and friends, who were also giving their best wishes and saying goodbye.

When the bride saw her, she cut through the crowd and gave Aimee a big hug.

"I am so happy you came. Thank you for being part of our special day."

"It was absolutely enchanting. Please tell your parents for me I think it was the most beautiful wedding. And the reception? Well, it's just over the top. Completely over-the-top. Thank you for the invite. We had a good time."

They hugged one more time, Aimee said goodbye, and she nodded toward the group and then left. It was an awkward exit. The room suddenly felt oppressive, like a gauntlet or a walk of shame. She worried she'd burst out in tears before she reached the exit. The most ridiculous thing about it was that she had no idea what her tears were being shed for. She was just nervous, feeling things were about to spin out of control.

Finally, the cool evening air bathed over her face, and she took a deep breath, pausing to clear her head and face whatever was coming next.

The boys were leaning against the Jeep and, when they saw her, instantly sprang into action. Andy went around to the driver side, while Cory opened the front door for her. She struggled again to get up in the seat, and with Cory's assistance, she managed to do so without tearing her dress.

Cory pulled her seat belt around her and hooked it in place. Her nerves started to rattle when he didn't give her a kiss to her cheek or say anything at all. Andy gripped the steering wheel like it was a lifeline. She turned to say something to Cory, but found herself staring at the glass of the door's window. She heard Cory climb in behind her. Andy turned the key, and they took off.

Several minutes passed in silence. The longer things were quiet, the more fear began to constrict her breathing. She opened the window a crack to get some air. She was getting impatient.

"You want some heat or air?" Andy offered.

She saw some friendship there in his eyes before he expertly masked it.

"I'm okay. But I don't want to do this, sit here like this. Are we going to talk now or…"

"Not here." Cory's statement shook her.

"Maybe you could fix us some coffee at your place?" Andy said calmly. "That's what he means." He chanced a quick glance in his rear view mirror at Cory but then steadied his eyes on the road.

So this is how it is.

It wasn't fair, but she was going to have to wait nearly an hour before she knew anything at all. She mustered the courage to speak out again.

"I'm sorry, but this is just too weird. What happened? Can you prepare me for what you want to talk about?" she pleaded with Andy.

"Aimee, I really think it's better if the three of us sit down at your place. We have some things to iron out." Andy spoke these words without taking his eyes off the road.

"Fine." Aimee adjusted her seat and then straightened her skirts. She suddenly remembered that her mother used to do that all the time, especially if she was angry or annoyed.

She could do this, whatever it was.

AIMEE SUDDENLY AWOKE, startled that she fell asleep. The car had stopped, parked in her driveway. She didn't wait for Cory, struggling but successfully extricating herself from the passenger seat. Grabbing her purse and scarf, she led the delegation to her front door.

Her eyes began to water, and her fingers shook, making it difficult to find her key. At last, she located it and let herself in. The two men closed the door behind them.

Her feet were sore.

"I have to get these shoes off. Help yourself to anything in the refrigerator. I'll be right out."

Sitting on her bed, she removed the jeweled sandals and rubbed her toes, noticing she had several blisters. In her bare feet, she made it back to the kitchen to make some coffee.

Andy and Cory had been whispering but quickly parted when she appeared. Cory had removed his jacket, but Andy kept his on.

"Anything else other than coffee?" she asked.

Andy shook his head no.

"No, thanks, Aimee," said Cory.

She got three mugs down from the upper cabinet, poured half-and-half into two of them, and then poured coffee into all three. She gathered everything together, joining the men in her cozy living room, and placed the mugs on her coffee table.

"I made yours black, Cory."

"Perfect."

Andy reached forward and thanked her for his mug while Aimee sat back, crossed her legs and waited. The warm coffee tasted heavenly.

Cory and Andy shared a look, and then Cory began. He turned to face her.

"So, Aimee, I've got some things I need to tell you."

"I'm all ears, Cory." She didn't like the way it came out but didn't feel like apologizing.

"I've not been completely honest with you."

Aimee inhaled and waited for it, whatever it was. She already knew she wasn't going to like it. But her goal was to get through the evening without bursting into tears. She was hoping she was overreacting.

"Okay. Let's get this over with," Aimee whispered.

"Andy brought some things to my attention, and I thank him for that," Cory said tentatively.

Aimee sent a frozen glare at Andy, her impatience flooding her mood.

"Look, Cory. Let's just get this over with, whatever it is. Have I done something wrong? Have I misread something? Did I offend either of you?"

Both men were quick to answer no.

Cory continued. "I received word that I was accepted to a program, a burn specialty course in Texas. I had applied for this before you and I met. And I didn't tell you that I've been in negotiations with them over the past few days."

"Well, isn't that good news? More training is good, right?" She was seeking some ray of hope, first from Cory and then Andy, but got none.

She was confused why there was so much sadness and regret in Cory's communication.

"Yes. It is good news. I was worried about my position on the Teams. I think you knew that."

Aimee nodded.

"But there's more. I've been hiding some things from you, Aimee, and I've been thinking that I should get some help with my alcohol and drug use."

She was beginning to sense the problem ahead of her.

"So that one bottle I found wasn't the only one, then? What you're saying is you've been taking painkillers, is that it?"

"Yes. And some other things too. I've been having trouble sleeping. And I've not been—"

Aimee could see he was struggling with his words.

"Just say it, dammit." Aimee was starved for the facts of his situation.

"I've also been seeing other women."

"What?" She stood. She wanted to throw her mug of coffee at him. She backed up from the table, suddenly not wanting to be around either man. "You son of a bitch. When did this start?"

Cory remained seated, his body posture was completely deflated. Aimee could also tell that Andy wished he could be anywhere else but in this room.

"It isn't about *when* it started, Aimee. It never

stopped. That's the truth of it. It's part of my addiction. They didn't mean anything, I swear. I just wanted to start telling you the truth. Telling everyone the truth of what I've become. I'd like to earn back your trust and love some day."

Aimee had heard her fill and wanted the words to stop. Her firewall came up to shield her, as it always did. Suddenly, there was no place to hide, no protection except behind that wall. What she'd thought was her world was in fact an illusion. She had to get to safer ground, and fast.

"I want you both out of this house immediately. I want you to go away and leave me alone. I don't want to see you guys—either of you."

She knew it was not what she'd intended to say, but she wanted the conversation to stop until she could hear it. Right now, it was too much to think about.

"Aimee," Andy interceded. "What Cory is trying to tell you is that he's sorry. And he's asking for your understanding and your help. He's going to need all of our help, if he gets clean. I know he loves you."

Andy's eyes were arched, his forehead lined with worry as she looked down on him seated before her. But it was not inside her to forgive anything right now. Her stomach was churned. Her brain was shouting, scolding her for being such a fool. Once more everything she thought was good about her world was gone.

And the worst thing about it was she didn't know if it *ever* had been real. How could she trust her judgment going forward? What was important right now was not to show weakness for the sake of her own pride. She wouldn't let them have that satisfaction.

"Well, thank you for the information." She allowed herself to enjoy the ice water in her veins and drew courage from it, pacing back and forth in front of them. "It's impossible for me to understand how you could think any of this would be okay with me. I feel used, taken advantage of. And Andy, apparently you knew about all this, and didn't tell me, which means you were in on it all along."

"I didn't know all of it, Aimee, I swear."

"You're asking me to believe that?"

"I understand. I'd probably feel the same way. But there were two paths and only one leads to getting healthy. Keeping secrets is the unhealthy path."

She wanted to slap him for not being honest earlier, for not giving her warning. She'd bought into the old Boy's Club routine she'd heard about with the Teams because she thought she could trust them. She was angry that she'd allowed herself to feel attraction for him, for perhaps playing into their little scheme. Was Andy the substitute? Was that the plan between them? Was that why he came out to Florida? She was filled with conspiracy theories running fast and loose through her head.

So, it all came down to trust. She didn't even trust herself, her feelings, or her judgment now.

"Andy's right. This is all on me, Aimee," said Cory.

"That's all right," she interrupted. "I think I've heard enough. I'd like to be alone now." She adjusted her tone's volume down, softening her request. "Please."

Cory stood, approaching her with his arms open, ready to embrace her one last time. She moved to the side.

"Don't touch me. You have got some nerve!"

"Aimee, please believe me. I am so very sorry. I never meant to hurt you. I hope some day you'll believe me, honey. It's my fault. I let things get out of control and I hurt the one person I cared about the most. I lost my nerve, and I lost my way. I'm going to work hard to get my honor back. I'm hoping that going to Texas will help me do that. I need to get well. This is not fair to you. I'm sorry."

"You're damned right it's not fair. But I'm done with this." Aimee walked to her front door and opened it. "I'm completely done. I have nothing more I need to hear, and I don't want to tell you all the things I'm feeling right now, because you don't deserve it, you asshole."

Cory grabbed his jacket in anger and was out the

front door in seconds. Andy lingered in the doorway for a minute.

"I'm sorry, Aimee, for my part in all this. I completely understand how you might feel I'm responsible for this, and I am but not in the way you're thinking. I want you to know that you didn't cause this. You deserve so much more."

He was going to continue, but Aimee stopped him. "No, Andy. Maybe it isn't your fault, but this is something you can't fix. I'm angry because I think you're the reason he's leveled with me. I should thank you for it, but right now I'm angry as hell. Please don't disrespect me by trying to take that away from me, okay? I don't need fixing."

"I understand, really I do. Call me if you want to talk."

"Are you nuts, Andy? Get out of my sight!"

With that, he turned and headed back to the Jeep. She watched them drive away then slammed the door, picked up the three partially consumed mugs on the coffee table, and placed them carefully in the kitchen sink, overruling the urge to smash them on the ground, or throw them at Andy's Jeep.

She was going to take a shower and go to bed but then remembered her little routine. These routines were going to be very important now until she could get to the space where she could fully accept what just happened. She was going to go through the motions of being alive, taking time for her runs, and enjoying the sunsets at the beach.

The beach heals everything.

She was counting on that big time.

Aimee did one more check of the windows and doors, making sure she was as safe as she could be. She checked her father's .38 in her bedside table, confirming that it was still loaded. She unzipped the side zipper on her skirt, unhooked the bodice of her top and carefully hung them on their special padded satin hanger in her closet. She'd loved wearing the dress, and that was real. She vowed that, someday, she would feel like wearing these beautiful things again.

She removed her under clothes and her pearls, turned on the shower, and stepped inside. After the warm spray hit her face, she allowed herself to finally cry.

The worst was over. Now she had to think about pulling her life back together, frame by frame. Memories of their happy times only solidified her resolve that what had been going on from her side was real.

And she was never going to let someone like Cory hurt her ever again.

CHAPTER 11

ANDY WAS DETERMINED to pack his bags and take off for a motel, flying home as soon as he could arrange it. At least, that was the plan he'd devised as he drove them both back to Cory's.

But he worried about leaving Cory alone and didn't trust that Cory would be safe. If his friend had been on one of his California Teams, he knew there were a couple of people he could call. But he didn't know anybody on Team 4 or any of the liaisons. He considered calling his LPO, Kyle Lansdowne, to get some advice. The one thing he was most concerned about was setting into motion something that would interfere with Cory's future.

Of course, Cory had done a pretty damn good job of screwing that up himself. Andy didn't like secrets and thought there was a possibility Cory could be a danger to himself. He would never forgive himself if that happened.

He followed Cory inside the house, hoping they could air out some of the bad blood he knew existed between them. Andy didn't want to leave with things raw and bloody between them. He also wondered how many of the promises he'd made Aimee that Cory really intended to keep. He had to find that out first.

Cory collapsed into the couch.

"So what do you think of your fucking good idea now, Andy?"

Cory's bitterness infused the room with tension. And he knew it was a dangerous sign. His conscience was telling him he needed to call the cops or take him somewhere.

"I'm not happy with how it went. You know that. But I understand how she feels. Cory, you know it was gonna happen anyway. I think if you get yourself…"

"I'm not listening to you anymore. I want to get my shit together and take off, get out of this fuckin' place."

"How about we'll talk about it tomorrow. But right now…"

Cory jumped to his feet and began to pace the room in front of him, then abruptly stopped. "Do you want to stay here? You go right ahead. I've got the place paid up for another few weeks. You should take it. You go live my life. Go take my girl, too, while you're at it."

"It's not like that, Cory. Don't you see that *you*

caused this?"

"I know you're right," Cory walked up to stand a foot away from Andy's body. It was a dangerous and reckless move. "I just don't fucking wanna hear it anymore."

"Maybe I should stay here tonight and make sure you're settled. Or, I also could call somebody and let you be somebody else's problem. Get law enforcement involved? Not sure that would be a good idea, but if I have to, I will. But I don't know who to call. I'm fresh out of ideas. So you tell me, should I call the cops? Should I call your LPO? Is there somebody else I should call?"

He didn't back up but stood his ground, waiting for Cory to back down. He wanted to see if he could do it, to show him that he had some kind of control over his behavior. He added more ammunition.

"The way I see it, Cory, is that you're not thinking straight. You've gotten your head screwed up and you're not thinking like yourself anymore. I wouldn't trust any decision of yours right now, and most certainly not tonight."

Cory moved away slowly and turned, looking out the window to the water beyond.

Andy added. "It's stress, man. You had a shitty deployment, and that could happen any time to any of us. And it does. But you can think about all that tomorrow when you've gotten some rest."

Andy was rewarded with a sneer followed by a glance to the refrigerator, and he knew Cory considered getting a beer. He vowed to stop him if he had to.

Cory ripped off his jacket and threw it on the ground. "God dammit."

"You got to get out of your fucking head man. Whatever you're thinking, it's fantasyland. We'll get real tomorrow. Tonight you go straight to bed.

Cory sat on the couch and slumped over his knees. "Everybody I know is at Little Creek. I start calling up there and I won't have a career."

"Maybe you don't have one now. You gotta do what's right for you. And I'm worried about you. We do it one bite at a time. I'll stay over tonight to make sure you're in bed and safe."

Cory looked up at Andy, tears streaming from his eyes. "I don't have anybody."

Andy took a seat across from his best friend. He tried to think of anyone he'd run across who had found themselves in this position. He knew about a couple of guys who had gotten jacked for selling equipment and guns, trying to make a little extra money on the side. It was a horrible violation of everything they stood for. The Navy had taken swift justice on those men, including jail time. A few of the regulars who knew about it were also busted for not informing the Navy.

But this was different. And he knew he had an obligation to make sure that a damaged and wounded soldier somehow didn't get put back on a Team where he could cause himself or others harm from the mental distraction. But Andy was just out of resources.

And even if he could walk away, the Navy would not take kindly if he didn't report it. And that was the rub. Andy knew he was involved up to his eyeballs. If he could just get Cory into some kind of a program, maybe he could work things out.

"You need to hit the bed. We'll begin sorting some of this out tomorrow morning. But you go to bed, and get some rest. I don't want you to take or use anything tonight, you hear me?"

Cory nodded. "Yeah. That's probably best."

"I'm going to sleep out here. Do you have drugs in your room?"

"Yeah, I do."

"Do I have to go through your room and clean out your drawers? Do you have a weapon here?"

"I'll get my little stash and bring it out to you. I didn't bring my Sig."

Andy packed up his clothes and set the duffel next to the couch. He was amazed he had stopped thinking about how much his feet hurt. He sat down and removed his shoes, knowing what he was going to find.

He gingerly peeled his socks off and stared down at

huge red blisters. He'd known it was a mistake. The whole evening was a mistake.

Trying to live someone else's life again.

Who were they kidding? They'd gone out, bought new suits and shoes, and tried to act the part of what? Some billionaire's kid? And for what? A few fancy hors d'oeuvres and some free booze? The whole idea suddenly felt ridiculous. It was a grown up costume party.

He was happiest at the beach—eating ice cream, screaming his lungs out in a race with big fat tires, and dodging all the other normal people in the world he had been tasked to protect. Not to take from or fawn all over rich people who didn't really care who he was. None of those girls who came after Cory cared anything about him. That was what was so sad. He was a piece of meat, a conquest. The price was too high.

He slipped off his suit pants and jacket, folded them neatly, and tucked them into his duffel bag. He placed his shoes underneath the rest of the contents, resting on the bottom. He was going to sleep in his red, white, and blue boxers.

Cory brought him a baggie filled with seven or eight pill bottles, a pipe of some kind, something black and tarry looking, and a small baggie filled with dried buds. Andy tossed the bag on the couch behind him.

"We're going to talk about this in the morning. I'm

gonna sleep here, on the couch, just to make sure you stay settled for the night. You try to go get a beer and I'm gonna be in your face, Cory. I'm doing this because I care for you, man. We're brothers, and I would hope you'd do the same for me. But don't go jumping on our friendship, man. Don't test me, Cory, because I want what's good for you almost more than I want anything else. You're not gonna be able to stop me, so don't even try."

"I appreciate that. You're a good friend. You're my only friend, and we're brothers."

Cory turned to go into the bedroom, and Andy called out to him. "Cory, come here."

The two men briefly hugged, ending with quick pats on the back. Andy held him at arm's length gripping his right shoulder and shaking him. "I'm pulling for you, Cory. We'll get through this, somehow."

He watched Cory disappear into the bedroom. Andy waited until he saw the lights turn out, before grabbing a blanket and pillow from his bedroom, laying them out on the couch. He picked up the bag Cory had given him, and walked out onto the patio. He set aside the firepit grate, and pushed the old charcoal to the sides. He found some tin foil in the kitchen and lay it in a double layer on the floor of the pit.

He tossed the baggie on top, poured lighter fluid on

it, and set it on fire, careful to step aside from the black, acrid smoke. The last thing he did was replace the grate on top and watched until the contents were reduced to ash. He heard a tiny ping and figured the glass pipe had exploded.

Inside, he hung by the large picture window and realized the moon was still shining, sending silvery shimmers to the calm ocean. He wondered if maybe Cory had called him as a cry for help. Maybe this was all supposed to happen this way. It wouldn't be the first time he'd missed an accurate assessment of the situation.

And it certainly wouldn't be the last.

Things had worked out much differently than he'd expected. He'd caught a couple glimpses of what he didn't want. He didn't want Cory's path. He didn't want that crowd he saw at the reception. He didn't want ever again to have to hurt the feelings of a woman who had only shown him respect and friendship, who was perhaps too trusting. Based on what he'd seen of the world, he thought he knew better. He couldn't fix the whole insane world. He could only do one thing at a time, and do that right.

He would stand for Cory for now. He'd let the beach and sand in Coronado take care of the rest.

As he lay back on the pillow and wrapped the coverlet over him, he thought about Aimee. He hoped she would be okay, and hoped she'd find a way to forgive. He was sad that his choices were so limited. If circumstances were different, Aimee would be just the kind of woman he could cherish.

Dwelling on that or what she thought of him was of no use, and was too self-serving. But it didn't stop him from feeling sad for what would never be.

CHAPTER 12

AIMEE WOKE UP early, her body ready for her normal six-thirty run on the beach. She dragged her legs over the edge of the bed and sat hunched over with her chin in her hands. She didn't feel like running. She felt like staying in her pajamas all day and watching sad romance movies and crying her eyes out.

"My whole life is a bad movie," she muttered.

Aimee stood and stretched, raising her fingers to the ceiling and then dropping down to touch her toes. She messed up her hair, rubbed her scalp, and then sifted it all back into place. She walked into the bathroom and was horrified with the woman she saw in the mirror.

Her eyes were nearly shut from puffiness, the results of the crying she did every time she woke up. Mascara had slipped down and created two dark wells underneath her eyes, streaked with tears. The black half-circles as well as faint traces of glittered eyeshadow were the only visible remnants from her Cinderella pumpkin ride last night.

She splashed water on her face, brushed her teeth, and brushed her hair, putting it back into a ponytail. She wore a baseball cap so she wouldn't have to show off her puffy eyes.

Then Aimee slipped off her pajama bottoms and her IRB tee shirt before she donned her sleek black running pants and lavender fleece top. She carefully put Neosporin on her blisters, and then covered them with anklet socks. She carefully slid into her green Nikes after making sure they were laced extremely loose.

Taking a water bottle from the refrigerator, she tucked it into her back pocket, opened her sliding glass door, and stepped out into the foggy morning. Carefully, she made her way through the sand dune and then down to the beach. She found it completely deserted. It was often like this on a Sunday morning. But this morning was unusually cold and uncharacteristically foggy, so she figured most of the tourists stayed away until the sun came out.

She'd have the beach mostly to herself. That was a good thing.

The ocean looked gray. The sunrise had left the sky purple, turning to yellow-orange in streaks that would soon disappear. She stretched briefly, set her watch for thirty minutes, and then headed down her usual course, finding the firm sand closest to the surf.

Images of last night danced through her head. She took it as a good sign she could still bear to think about her red dress, the smell of the flowers, and the lavish decorations. How it felt to slow dance next to someone warm who had powerful arms. She was happy for the young bride and hoped they were happy as a couple. She also trusted that the bride knew how lucky she was.

The bicycle twins passed her, their silver hair blowing in the breeze. She waved and gave them a warm smile, which they returned.

Later on, she found a group of women running together in a pod in the opposite direction. All of them wore pink, and one of the women had no hair. Aimee gave the group a thumbs-up, and she got seven or eight in return.

She passed a heavyset woman walking alone, snuggled in a ski jacket with a checkered scarf around her neck. She passed two men who sat on collapsible stools, fishing.

When her alarm went off, she saw the path that led down to Connie's restaurant. At some point, she'd go back there. But not yet. She wasn't quite ready yet.

She headed for home.

She knew at some point she had passed Cory's house. Aimee was proud that she didn't even try to look for it or to see if anyone was awake. She was focused on the stretch of beach in front of her, the way her lungs filled with air, and the sparkle of the pristine, white crystal sand.

As the sky became more blue, she noticed the heat of the day starting. The fog was gone, and one by one, people came out from the houses and beach trails along the shore, to play, to walk, to just be there.

Aimee knew she was close to her house when she spotted the abandoned pink house five houses down from hers. She'd always wondered about that house. No one ever sat outside on the patio, or came out on the balcony on the second floor. The windows were boarded up. The paint peeled and part of the rain gutter on the side had come undone, hanging at an angle at the side, ready to fall down completely.

The house appeared abandoned.

On a whim, she ran up and over the dunes and then carefully trudged through the seagrass. Hopping over the shallow drainage canal, she walked up the nearly deteriorated wooden steps to the patio. A barbecue had been turned on its side, the contents spilled. Two rusty lawn chairs sat side-by-side in perfect view of the ocean. She walked along the side of the house to see if she could find any window not covered in plywood.

Aimee found a door open, leading to a storage

room, which contained an old freezer. A dirty mop had been stuck inside, propping up the lid. Just past the freezer was a door which, remarkably, was open.

Stepping inside a large kitchen area, a small sliver of light coming from a hole in the plywood cover made the room barely visible. All the appliances had been torn out, or removed and left broken in the dining room. The refrigerator door was left ajar. The huge L-shaped countertop was made of 1940's vintage pink and black tile, in somewhat decent condition except for the cracked and dark moldy grout lines.

She walked into the living room and discovered she could open the front door, which let in more light. That enabled her to walk the stairs up to the clutter of broken furniture and dirty old mattresses littering the three bedrooms there. Both bathrooms were also done in four inch green tiles, trimmed in black. Someone had removed a bathtub in one bathroom, and both toilets were missing as well.

As she came down the stairs, she imagined a home decorated in pastels, pictures of beach scenes on the wall. Pillows with mermaids, starfish, and sand dollars brightened the white furniture. She saw people mingling on the patio and smelled a barbeque fired up sending delicious aromas.

She took pictures of several of the rooms with her cell, and then closed the front door, making sure it was locked before exiting the doors through the storage area the way she'd let herself in. She decided to leave those doors as she found them—open.

Standing back on the beach, she was able to take one last picture, capturing both stories, and a portion of the yard in front.

What if I could turn this home into a showplace?

A project was definitely what she needed. And, if this house didn't work, perhaps it was time she started looking. Now there wasn't anything holding her back.

Walking back to her bungalow, she sat at the counter and reached for the pad of paper she kept there with a pen. Aimee made a list of all her questions, starting with who the owner was. From memory, she listed all the things that would have to be fixed, going room by room, looking over the pictures to make sure she didn't miss anything. Added to the list was finding contractors who she'd hire to do the work. She needed the name of a local Realtor to help her decide what it would be worth when she finished to see if it was even worth doing the project at all.

During her shower, she remembered the young man at JJ's who looked like her brother. That was another loose end she wanted to explore.

As she put moisturizer on her face and blow-dried her hair, the lady she saw in the mirror now didn't look anything like the wreck who had greeted her this morning. Even her eyes had started to lose their puffiness.

Her stomach began to call, so after getting dressed for a warm Florida fall day, she put on flip-flops, which would help with the blister healing and decided to go to JJ's for breakfast to see if she could find the kitchen helper she'd seen that night.

She called Shelley.

"Good timing. I was just going to cook some eggs. I'll meet you there in a half hour? Give me time to shower."

"Perfect."

AIMEE WAS FIRST to arrive and took a table in the corner by a large statue of a lobster holding a tray and wearing a tux. She'd seen tourists take their picture in front of it on many occasions.

Her server approached with the mug of coffee she'd ordered. "My friend will be here soon."

"Great, I'll come back then." The young server looked to be about high school age.

"Say, can I ask if the owner is here?"

"What's wrong?"

Aimee laughed. "Not to worry. Nothing's wrong. I just have a question about someone who works here."

"Who?"

"Well, do you know a Logan Greer? He'd be a little

older than I am."

The server cocked her head and considered the question. "I don't think we have anyone named Logan here, but I only work the early breakfast on weekends. They have a full staff at night, especially when they have entertainment."

"Yes, this was on Wednesday, I think. There was a band here. It was packed. That's the night I saw him."

"Well, the owner doesn't usually come in on Sundays, but even then, I'm not sure he's as familiar with the staff. We have a restaurant manager. He hires us and the bartenders and some of the kitchen staff. And we have a bookkeeper who does the payroll. She comes in on Mondays, so you'd have to catch her tomorrow. That's the only day she works. I don't know when Roger will be in, but his hours are not set."

"Would you be willing to give me their phone numbers?" Aimee asked.

"You just have to call the restaurant. I don't even have a way to reach them outside of work. But calling the restaurant would be your best bet."

Aimee pulled out her clipboard and asked for the manager's name as well as the name of the bookkeeper. "Thanks so much."

Shelley walked through the door, and Aimee gave her a wave. "Here's my friend now."

"Hi there," Shelley said, giving her a big smile.

"Would you like some coffee?" the server asked.

"I'd love some."

The young girl went in search of coffee. Aimee was anxious to tell Shelley about the house she found.

"I was running on the beach this morning, and I found this house that's very close to my place. It looks like it's abandoned. I walked through it and I took some pictures. Let me show you."

She placed her cell phone on the table and scrolled through several of the pictures, watching Shelley's expression. At first her friend was excited, but as she viewed the photos, her expression grew sour. She pushed the cell phone back across the tabletop.

"What do you think?" Aimee asked.

"Honestly?"

"Yes!"

"I think you've lost your mind. This place is a dump. I mean, this is a contractor's dream. Do you have any experience doing any of that work? This isn't just paint and carpet and drapes, you know?"

"I *do* know. I've got a list of things I need to find out about, and of course I need to figure out what it would cost. But wouldn't it be great?"

"Well, Aimee, you're talking a lot of money here. And if you have to hire a contractor to do it all, I'm not sure it would work out. I mean, this looks like a money pit."

Aimee could see there would be no convincing Shelley that what she was going to entertain was a good idea. But that wasn't gonna stop her.

"What does Cory think?" Shelley asked.

Her comment made Aimee freeze in place. All of a sudden, her world got small. She temporarily forgot the pain of last night, and all her former confusion came screaming back. Along with all the pain and the tears.

"I haven't told him yet." She couldn't make eye contact.

"Well, I think Cory would know some people. He'd certainly know much better than I. But I suppose he'll have to go back to Virginia, so I don't know how all that timing will work for you."

Aimee decided not to tell Shelley about her situation. "I'm just toying with the idea. I thought it would be fun to look at places, maybe invest in a little place here."

"Sure, I think that's a great idea. Do you have the down payment?"

"I have some from my parents. I just wasn't sure I wanted to buy something here."

"Well, we're not that far from Little Creek, or at least closer than you'd be in California. I guess it depends on where you want to live, Aimee. Have you thought about that? Have you and Cory made any plans?"

That comment caught her off guard. "No, no plans. There is just something about this place that feels good to me, Shelley. It's not perfect. But there's something about the beach—this beach, in particular—that makes me feel like it's home."

Aimee was a little fragile inside, and when she felt tears beginning to well up, she quickly grabbed her coffee and took several long sips.

The server brought Shelley's coffee and a refill for Aimee. They ordered. Then came the awkward silence Aimee was dreading.

"Is Andy still around?" Shelley asked.

"I suppose so. Why?"

"I was hoping that by now he would call me." Shelley tilted her head and then looked up at Aimee. "Has he said anything? Anything about me?"

She didn't like lying to Shelley, but she had to.

"I'm sorry, but I really haven't had much communication with them. I've sort of left the two of them to be together. You know how it is."

"Yes, believe me, I do. But I just thought…"

"Sometimes I have a hard time understanding Cory."

Shelley nodded and drank her coffee. Aimee was glad that her friend didn't pry. She was positive that Shelley picked up that something strange was going on.

"If I see him again before he leaves, I'll tell him we spoke."

Shelley beamed. "Thank you."

CHAPTER 13

Andy made coffee, trying to stay quiet enough to keep Cory sleeping. Pouring himself a cup, he drowned it in half-and-half, and then took the coverlet outside with him to sit on one of Aimee's chairs, watching the ocean.

The gray morning matched his insides, and even the coffee didn't do anything to change his mood. He wanted to go back to California as soon as he felt it was safe to do so. He was hoping Cory would be able to make contact with the people in San Antonio to get him set up.

He watched several beachcombers search for shells that had washed up during the night. The beach was nearly deserted. He sat back, closing his eyes and checking his insides.

Andy knew he should give his LPO a call. It was too early to do so for another few hours, but he decided, no matter what Cory's state of mind, that call would have to be made.

I should have left a message last night.

But last night, he'd been exhausted. He needed the rest just as much as Cory did. The lumpy couch was no substitute for a real bed.

As the sun rose behind him, he noticed more travelers on the beach. A dark form emerged from the distance and then crossed in front of the house. He would recognize those shoes anywhere. His heart skipped a beat as he did the only thing he could do, just watch as she came into view and then slipped back into the fog and out of his life.

It wasn't numbness but the costume, the mask he wore to hide emotions he needed to push back. It wasn't that he lacked caring. He cared too much and didn't have the capacity to do anything about it.

This wasn't the time for second-guessing.

HE MUST HAVE fallen asleep, because he heard the sliding glass door open behind him, as he jerked fully awake and discovered he had a stiff neck. It had gotten considerably warmer, and now the sky was bright blue. He figured he must have slept slumped in the chair for an hour or more.

Cory leaned over and picked up his spilled coffee. "You want a refill?" he asked as he held the mug up.

"Sure. Thanks, Cory."

Andy wondered now if the vision of Aimee running down the beach wasn't just a dream he'd had.

Cory was shirtless, wearing only polar bear flannel pajama bottoms. His hair was splayed all over his head, growing like tufted sea grass, and he yawned as he leaned over and gave Andy the warm mug.

"You look like shit."

Andy figured he deserved that.

"Look at you, ToolTime. Got your jammies on, I see."

Cory grinned, curling his arms and flexing his pectoral muscles. "We're the pair, aren't we?"

Andy sipped his coffee. It was bitter and too overheated.

"What the hell is that?" Cory was pointing to the tin foil and ashes in the fire pit.

"That's hopefully the last of your bad habits, Cory. I forgot to clean up." Andy removed the grate, peeled the tin foil up at the edges, and rolled the whole thing into a hamburger bun-shaped blob. He excused himself to the kitchen, and disposed of it in the garbage.

"You just put about six hundred dollars up in smoke."

"Better than in your lungs and bloodstream, Cory. Sit. Can we work out your next move?"

Cory pulled the other Adirondack chair closer and

deposited himself. "I already made a call to San Antonio, but it's Sunday, and I'm not sure I'll hear back until tomorrow."

"Good. How do you feel?"

"I'm good. Feel like I've been eating garbage all night. My head hurts. I'm guessing it will really start hurting as the day goes on." He was tracing the top of the coffee mug with his forefinger. "And I even called a guy I know who's in a twelve-step program. A former Team Guy."

Andy was impressed. "That's a smart move."

"He's offered to take me to a meeting. What do you think?"

"That's the kind of friend you need right now, Cory. I don't have any experience with these programs, but a lot of guys get help there. Gals too. We aren't the only ones."

"He says there's a meeting tonight I can go to. Do you want to go with?"

"No thanks. I think that's something you two should do together."

"Okay, so if I do, will you be here when I get home? Or are you leaving?"

"I can stay. I didn't make any plans or change my flights home yet. Let's find out what's going on with San Antonio, and then I'll decide."

"Fair enough. Can I ask you another question?"

"Shoot."

"Have you ever heard about other guys like me? I mean, what did they do for help?"

"I'm guessing the answer to that is a resounding yes, but the old guys would be your best bet. I think your former Team Guy would be a great place to start. I'm not really qualified to answer. Only thing I'm here for is to make sure you stay willing to change. I don't have any special potion or advice. You're the one going to do the work, if you want it enough, Cory. If you were in California, I have a couple of guys I'd have you call. But not out here."

Cory had a craving for pancakes smothered in syrup, so he directed Andy to his favorite Samoan pancake house where they stocked up on carbs. When they returned home, Cory got the call from San Antonio. The Joint Base San Antonio-Fort Sam Houston Burn Center had facilities for him to stay right on the hospital grounds. They also had an outpatient drug and alcohol treatment clinic privately contracted by specialty physicians both inside and outside the military community. The services would be free to him as long as he was enrolled in the special training. Best of all was that there were counselors available nearly any time of the day or night.

Cory offered to fly out as soon as his paperwork came through, and they indicated that, if he flew out sooner, rather than wait the two to four weeks for the Navy to process it, he'd have a room and could begin class with the rest of the group who were due to start the following week.

And they said they'd take care of the final sign-off for his injury, as long as he didn't have any complications.

Andy loaned him the money to catch a plane the next day.

"You remember what I said about my bank account, Cory? I used all my savings on special equipment I purchased for the trip to Africa. I gotta have this back."

"I'll return every penny. Not sure I can do it right away, but I'll pay you back."

"Then I say go with my blessing. Make the most of your opportunity. It's going to get tough, but hang in there."

When Cory's friend arrived, Andy was introduced. The former SEAL was a scary looking dude. He stood about three inches taller, nearly outweighing both Cory and Andy together. He looked more like a former NFL player. His arms were covered in colorful tats with scary dragons, snakes and fanged demons. It was obvious the man had pulled himself out of some kind of Hell. Andy was glad he'd decided not to go with them, but he knew Cory would be safe.

"I hope I'll be crashed. Looking forward to going to bed early to catch up on my sleep." To the big guy, Andy nodded, "Thanks."

"No problem, brother."

Andy watched them leave. Cory climbed into the passenger side of a black custom monster truck. The engine rattled all the windows of the house as Cory was chauffeured away in a cloud of smoke.

Remembering the truck at JJ's, Andy chuckled.

"Say hello to Phyllis."

He was still shaking his head, laughing, as he walked out on the sand, not wanting to miss the sunset. He worshiped dying sun like everyone else who had come out that night.

It was spectacular.

CHAPTER 14

Aimee's Monday morning run was easier than yesterday's. Convinced that routine and staying busy would help heal the wounds and disappointments of her heart, she showered, grabbed some yogurt for breakfast, and drove down to JJ's, hoping to see either the restaurant manager or the bookkeeper.

She had left a phone message for both of them.

The Monday morning crowd wasn't anything like Sunday, and she nearly had the restaurant to herself. She ordered coffee and a bowl of oatmeal and waited for the manager to come join her at the table.

Mr. Roger Valdez was a very trim man in his late forties, with a pencil thin mustache and dark black, curly hair. He spoke with an accent Aimee thought was either Cuban or South American.

"What can I do for you?" he said as he pulled up a chair across the table from her.

"Mr. Valdez, I was here last week on Wednesday

night, and I saw two people in the parking lot. One of them resembled my brother, who has been missing for about seven years. I came to ask for your help, if you're able."

"This person was a guest?"

"No, I think he works here."

"We have a lot of turnover here, Miss Greer, is it?"

"Yes, but you can call me Aimee."

"Can I ask your brother's name, please?"

"Logan Greer."

Valdez sat back in his chair, folding his arms over his lap, tapping his four fingers on his left upper arm. "Like I said, we must go through probably three hundred, maybe four hundred people a year. The restaurant business is not very skilled, and we get college students who are in transit, people just passing through in all circumstances. A very transient crowd, I must say. It's difficult to find someone who will stay long-term. But I honestly do not remember his name."

"I understand your bookkeeper, Mrs. Jackson, works today?"

"Yes." He checked his watch. "She arrives, in about thirty minutes, if you can wait."

"Would it be possible for you to check your records?"

"Yes, we can do this. However, I have to wait for Mrs. Jackson first. She has all the files."

"The two men I saw in the parking lot were arguing. One was a rather short, heavyset man. The other one, possibly my brother, was tall and thin. They were having some kind of an argument, and when I called his name, both of them disappeared in opposite directions."

"So he didn't wait on you, or you didn't see him in the restaurant?"

"No, but they both wore white jackets. They looked like kitchen help. Perhaps cooks?"

Valdez crossed his legs and slapped his knee. "The kitchen staff. This is our biggest problem. I have an extremely volatile head cook, and many of our helpers find they can only tolerate him a little. I have tried very hard to explain things to Sergio, but this is his world. He is my only long-term employee, and the owner has made me promise that he will never be fired."

"Is he a bit heavy and not tall?"

"Yes, it sounds like him. I have seen him fire people before in the parking lot."

"So when does your cook arrive then?"

"Well, some of them are here now. And they are doing prep for dinner already. I think our Sergio doesn't like to get up with the sun. It will be noon. If you come back then, you'll be able to talk to Mrs. Jackson as well."

"Thank you for your time."

Aimee shook the managers hand and wrote down notes on her tablet. She had about three hours to kill so decided to take a drive to the Tax Collector's office and do some research on the pink house.

Memories of Saturday night floated through her head, reminding her how she felt during the silence of the car on their way back to Aimee's house. This time, as she passed through several little beach towns along Gulf Boulevard, each one taking less than five minutes to drive through, she was in a different frame of mind. But she wondered if Andy had left for California. Or perhaps he took Cory to Texas on his way back.

She decided it would be a good idea to try writing down signs of houses that were for sale. She also needed a Realtor recommendation so she could familiarize herself with the market and prices.

Aimee passed multiple ice cream shops and two-story beach stores that sold everything from inflatable flamingos to boogie boards, bathing suits, and beach towels. She drove past the bicycle rental spot and one of her favorite ice cream shops that made the best Cuban sandwiches she'd ever tasted.

The Tax Collector's office shared a building with the Public Works Department. It was next door to City Hall, also in shared quarters.

Inside, a row of file cabinets lined one wall. On top of the last one was an oscillating fan, silently circulating air. A cheap radio played country music in the background. The office appeared to have two employees, both seated behind metal desks.

An attractive woman with black cat-eyes glasses, studded with rhinestones, looked up and asked, "Can I help you?"

"Yes, I'd like to find out the owner's name and address of a piece of property."

"You have the address?"

"Yes, right here." Aimee didn't want to shout the address across the room because she knew, with the town being so small, her chances of keeping her inquiry a secret were greatly diminished.

She held up her tablet to show the woman, who approached the counter, turned the tablet around, and then wrote the address on a slip of paper. "I'll be right back."

Aimee searched the walls, covered with local artist photographs, watercolors and oil paintings depicting various places around Sunset Beach. She noticed photographs of the dog park, a beach access bridge made of wood, the surf, and the sand dunes. She also saw a cluster of small oil paintings done in plein-air style, depicting small bungalows, brightly colored, and trimmed in equally bright contrasting colors. Examining one of the tags, she saw they were part of a local artist's collective, like the paintings at Connie's.

The attractive blonde woman had been combing through pages in a black three-ringed binder. She clicked it open, removed a small sheaf of papers and brought them up front.

"I'm afraid you'll have to show identification, and I will make you copies of these pages, but they are a dollar apiece."

"How many do you have?" Aimee asked, presenting her California driver's license.

The woman counted the pages scrolling at the upper right with thin fingers.

"I count thirteen."

Aimee opened her purse again and produced a credit card.

The woman shook her head. "I'm sorry, we only take cash."

Any produced a twenty dollar bill.

"I'm sorry, we don't have change."

From across the room the other woman spoke up. "Oh heaven's sake, Sylvia, I've got the change." She lay a ten and two fives on the counter. "That's the best I can do, sorry."

Aimee handed her the twenty. Then she gave the blonde woman fifteen. "Perhaps you can apply the change to your library fund," Aimee whispered.

Without answering, the blonde woman turned on her heel and brought the papers to a large copy machine and then returned with Aimee's copies.

Anxious to read the records, she sat.

The legal papers were confusing, but it appeared there was a living trust that had ownership, on behalf of a woman who lived in Sarasota. From the tax records, the trust had been created some twenty years ago by a man, whose address was listed as the property.

How could that be?

She knew that she might have to contact the attorney handling the trust and perhaps try to go search out this woman, Carmen Hernandez.

Checking her watch, Aimee realized it was time to return to JJs. She folded the paperwork, tucked it in her purse, and headed back south along the Boulevard.

This time, the restaurant was filled with people on lunch break. She looked for Mr. Valdez and waved to him once they made eye contact. He motioned for her to follow.

They climbed a narrow stairway leading to a tiny office cluttered with papers, boxes of more papers, and shelves stacked with papers. Aimee thought it looked like a hamster lived there, or at least someone adverse to filing.

Hunched over her desk and buried in a handwritten ledger, was an attractive African-American woman, who wore her hair short, and dyed bright orange. Even her fingernails were painted orange.

When Mr. Valdez introduced her, Mrs. Jackson smiled, revealing even her lipstick was orange.

"You the nice lady who left me that sweet message?"

"Yes, ma'am."

"Well, Mr. Valdez says that this particular man was working here last Wednesday?"

"Yes, that's when I saw him. He was in the parking lot, and there was some kind of an argument going on."

Mrs. Jackson rolled her eyes and let her fingers flutter through the air. "That kind of thing happens all the time here. Mr. Sergio runs them out the back door almost as fast as we take them in."

"Yes, Mr. Valdez told me."

Valdez needed to get back to the floor. "Everything okay here?"

"Right as rain. I'll send her down in a couple of minutes." She closed her ledger. "So Mr. Valdez says your brother's been missing for more than seven years?"

"Yes. When my parents were alive, they tried multiple times to find him. He's originally from California." Aimee looked around the room for a chair to sit.

"Just take those boxes off that chair over there and put them on the floor. I'm sorry, I should've offered it to you." Her face showed concern. "Let me ask you this, do you have a picture of your brother?"

Aimee wasn't sure if she still had the family photograph she used to keep in her wallet all the time. "If I do," she continued to search the pockets of her billfold, "it was taken over ten years ago. Not sure you would recognize him now."

While Aimee continued to finger through cards, notes, receipts, and credit cards, Mrs. Jackson asked her, "So you haven't seen your brother in seven years, then? Has anybody seen him?" She'd pulled a manilla file out of her desk drawer, briefly opened it, but then covered it with her arms.

Aimee found the small picture, and carefully removed it where it had stuck to the back of her Social Security card. "Here we are. I was a sophomore in high school. He was a year ahead of me."

She handed the photograph to Mrs. Jackson.

"What a lovely family. You sure growed up nice. Your brother looks a lot like you." She leaned into the photograph and examined it more closely. "I'm thinking I've seen this boy. Of course, he's not a boy now."

Aimee's heart nearly leapt out of her chest. She had never hoped to find Logan, let alone find him here in Florida.

"So does he work here? Will he be coming in today?"

"I'm sorry, Aimee. I'm gonna have to refer you to the place where we get some of our helpers. I'm not supposed to give you much information, you know. It's the law. But I feel for you."

"What do you mean organization?"

Mrs. Jackson bit her lower lip, her eyes down cast.

"Please. I need to find him."

"Were you aware he's got problems?"

"Yes. That started not long after this picture was taken. He had a drug problem. Long history of drug problems."

"Okay, then. Well as far as coming to work today, I can tell you that's not happening. Apparently, if he's this boy, this man, I'm pretty sure he's the one that Sergio fired." She gave Aimee a long look before she said, "He came from a halfway house. It's a drug diversion program for drug offenses. Our owner likes to help those who can't help themselves, and we get a steady stream of these kids, men and ladies, and, well, many of them work out and go on to do other things. Over half of them don't make it. And I'm sorry to say, if he is your brother, he's one of the ones who didn't."

"Can you tell me where this halfway house is?"

"First of all, he doesn't use the name Logan Greer. I would probably get in a whole lotta trouble if I told you what name he used. But I can give you the name of the halfway house. Maybe he's still there."

Aimee hugged Mrs. Jackson, and she danced down the stairs, clutching the address of the Sunshine Palms rehab facility. She wasn't sure exactly what she was going to find, but now she knew that she might be able to connect with the remnants of her family.

She wasn't doing it for Logan or even for herself. She was doing it for her mom and dad.

CHAPTER 15

Andy and Cory left for the Tampa airport when it was still dark outside. He had a seven-thirty flight with one layover.

"If she asks, will you tell Aimee I made it? I'm going to Texas?"

"Of course I will. But she made it pretty clear how she wanted that to go."

"I'm just gonna keep it simple, Andy. This is going to be a really challenging course from what I've heard. But it should give me some good creds. I'm going to be a student-fiend, just focus on the work."

"And getting healthy."

"Absolutely. Put everything else out of my mind."

"I think that's wise. Take it a little chunk at a time, Cory. With nobody looking over your shoulder, don't go telling yourself you can have just one beer or some dumb shit. No creative thinking, okay?

"Right. Some of the stories I heard last night, they

started exactly like I've been doing. Some of these guys lost their houses, their families. A few of them even live under the freeway, and they still go to meetings."

"I think you should feel grateful. You let it slide one time, and then it starts all over again. You got to go back to zero."

"Well, I'm ready."

Andy pulled into short-term parking which got a reaction out of Cory. "You don't have to do that. Just drop me off at the curb."

"Nope. I'm making sure you're on that plane."

The airport was only half-open. Many of the airline kiosks were closed and the TSA lines were nonexistent. Cory checked one large suitcase and was handed his tickets. He threw his computer bag over his shoulder, and the two men hugged.

They parted at the entrance to the First Class line. Cory showed his military ID, and was shuttled to the front.

Andy lost track of him once he got through screening.

Andy muttered a little prayer for his safety. "Godspeed, Cory. Take the chance you're given. Don't fuck it up."

CORY HAD CONVINCED Andy to stay a little bit longer in the house. At first, all he wanted to do was go home and get someplace where it was familiar. He missed having bonfires on the beach with the guys, the workouts, and having beers at the Scupper.

The ride home was going to take more time, since it was a Monday and the traffic was heavy. He stopped to buy some breakfast and then continued back, headed at last toward the beaches.

Just like the first time he walked in, the picture window in the living room took his breath away. It had turned out to be a nice fall day after all, but rain was forecasted for tomorrow. He could see the huge gray clouds forming on the horizon.

He moved his duffel bag to the bed in the spare bedroom, then sat out on the patio and watched the water and the carnival of people walking by.

He decided to give Kyle Lansdowne, his LPO, a call.

"Hey, Andy, have you been good?"

"Not too good, thanks."

"I'm glad. You deserve a little R&R." After a brief silence, Kyle asked him why he was calling.

"I kind of ran into a situation here with Cory, and I wanted to run it by you."

"That's a shame. You two are close. Did you guys have a falling out?"

"Yes and no. It's complicated. I just wanted to make sure I handled it correctly."

"Okay, I'll see if I can help."

"Cory got himself jacked up on painkillers for his elbow fix, and to make matters worse, he was doing quite a bit of drinking. I didn't worry about it at first, because I didn't realize he was still using the pain pills. But he was drinking all day and would start right after breakfast. I got worried when I found out he was doing the pills too. That's when I had to draw the line."

"Ouch. Not good. What do you want from me?"

"I trust your judgment, Kyle. I just wanna know I did the right thing."

"Well, that depends, of course, on what you did."

Andy was annoyed with himself. It was a lot harder to talk to Kyle than he had anticipated.

"We had a pretty bad argument, and I pretty much got in his face and told him he needed to clean himself up, get some help or, I threatened to call the cops, which of course would get the Navy involved."

"I'll bet he didn't like that one bit."

Andy could hear Kyle's children in the background.

"Excuse me, Andy, I have to go break something up."

"Go right ahead." He listened while Kyle raised his voice, and after a quick discussion, several kids chattering at once, someone got a swift spank. Silence followed.

"I'm back. Christy's working today, so I'm watching the kids, and we have Danny's here too."

"No problem. Sounds like it got resolved."

"It did. It most definitely did."

"Anyway, I felt like a traitor, but I was worried he was going to do something dumb."

"Okay, so what happened?"

"I told him he should go check himself into somewhere and get some treatment. That's when he told me that he had applied to Burn School in San Antonio, and they accepted him."

"That's a good program. He was lucky to get in that one."

"Yeah, I thought so too. I really worried he'd blow the opportunity."

Andy watched as a little kid was riding on one of the fat tire bikes, and had the speed cranked up and was going too fast. Just as he predicted, the boy lost control when he got caught in the surf. The bike stopped, but he kept going, flipping end-over-end over the handlebars.

"I just saw a major wipeout with one of these beach bikes you can rent. The kid's going to be okay, though, it seems."

"You need to go check on him?"

"No, he had several adults chasing him to begin with.

"Got it."

"Anyway, I wasn't the only one he's been hiding things from. He had a really nice girl here, and she broke up with him, when she found out all the stuff he was doing. So, the long and short of it is, I shipped him off to San Antonio this morning. I paid for his ticket so he'd get there and have a room on the hospital campus. Apparently he can get some counseling and treatment there since he's enrolled in the school."

"Sounds like everything's going to sort itself out. I'd say you did good."

"I just want to know if I should have done more. Am I obligated to report this? I don't want the Navy breathing down my neck if they think I didn't bring it to someone's attention."

"You're doing that now, Andy. But I wouldn't worry about it. I mean, he's going to be in a hospital setting, a facility there where they can take care of him if he goes off the rails. They run a pretty tight ship. The Army doesn't take too kindly to SEALs messing up their program, so I think it would be dangerous to have someone intervene and give them advanced warning. Let them figure it out for themselves. He's going to be watched like a hawk. They'll bust him for anything, trust me."

Andy was relieved.

"Now, that's not to say he couldn't find somebody

to get in trouble with, but if he's motivated, he should be okay. It's not like he's been doing this for a couple of years or anything, right?"

"Right."

"I wouldn't punish yourself or overthink it. I think you helped him dodge a bullet. That's good on you."

"Thanks, Kyle."

"Do you want me to give you some referrals, see if I can get some names over at the joint base?"

"That would be good. Just in case."

"Good. I'll dig around and text them to you tomorrow. So how much longer are you staying?"

"I'm supposed to come back in about a week. It's beautiful here. But it's way different than California."

"Oh yeah, that's nice over there on the Gulf."

"I was thinking… Cory paid up rent through the end of next month on this house here. I was wondering if I could extend my time here a few days longer. What do you think?"

"You had a tough one, especially for your first tour. I can authorize an extra week, even two, if you need it. If you stay in shape, all you'd be missing here is a little bit of work up. We don't have our next assignment yet. So stay and get some of that beach time that you missed before. It's hard on a guy when you have to watch out for somebody else. You're a good friend. He's lucky to have you. I've had guys who nearly get killed worrying about someone else on a mission, always watching for them to do something stupid. Just kick back and enjoy it for a little while, and then come home."

"Thanks, Kyle. I really appreciate that. I'll let you know a couple of days ahead of time."

"No problem. Don't expect a limo at the airport or anything."

Andy chuckled. "Can you believe it? I was going to send the Team some oranges and you can't ship them to California. Did you know that?"

"I do now. Get lots of rest, kid. And get some running in, and get to the gym. You know the drill."

"Yes, sir, I do."

"And, Andy, go get laid. That's an order."

CHAPTER 16

AIMEE HAD CALLED ahead to the Sunshine Palms, and she was told that non-patients—even family members—were not allowed to visit without prior medical authorization. She tried to get herself an appointment with one of the counselors, but she kept getting stalled.

In the morning she was going to keep to her normal routine. She'd take her hour-long run along the beach, and then she was going to attempt a visit in person. She'd see if she could worm her way inside.

She'd tossed and turned all night long, unable to sleep. Even the cup of hot chocolate and a little romance TV at midnight didn't help. She tried to read, and her eyes wouldn't focus.

Taking a shower usually relaxed her, so she used her lavender shower gel that always left a soothing, gentle scent on her skin. She changed her pajamas to a fresh nightgown and finally was able to fall asleep.

Six o'clock in the morning came very early. She slipped on her black running pants, and her lavender fleece top. Placing her hair in a ponytail, she decided not to wear her baseball cap. She grabbed a water from the refrigerator, placing it behind her waist in the pocket, and headed to the door. When her feet touched the outside, she realized she'd forgotten to put on her shoes!

Back in the bedroom, she applied first aid cream to her blisters, gingerly covered them with ankle socks, and once again slipped into her green Nikes.

There was no fog today. Just a beautiful rose, purple, and orange sky, reflections of a sunrise happening behind her to the east. She set her watch for thirty minutes, and started her run.

There were several more people out this early, since it was supposed to be an extremely warm day. She greeted the two bicycle twins, and the woman's group running to strike a blow for breast cancer, again.

"Good going, ladies!" she shouted.

"You too!" they said, along with several virtual air high-fives.

A pair of older men were working near the water's edge with metal detectors. A young couple sat on one of the benches next to a beach access trail. An older couple walked hand-in-hand.

In the distance, she saw the dark outline of someone sitting on the sand, watching the waves. As she approached, he turned his head in her direction, and she instantly recognized Andy.

She nearly stumbled, so surprised. Her left foot crossed over her right, and she lost her balance for a second. He was on his feet in a flash, but she'd already righted herself and didn't need assistance.

"What are you doing here?" she asked.

"I'm at Cory's for a few days more. I don't want to interfere with your run, but can I join you?"

Aimee felt her cheeks and neck turn blotchy red, like what always happened when she was nervous. Her swarm of buzzing butterflies set up a vibration in her chest that caused her breathing to hitch.

"Okay, let's go," she agreed.

Aimee resumed her somewhat faster pace, and he stayed right next to her, matching her stride in tandem. There were so many things running through her mind as she tried to focus on the crunch of shells beneath her feet, the sounds of the waves crashing on the beach, and the faint calling of birds. But she also couldn't help but hear his heavy breathing.

What she'd been most afraid of, came true. He knew what he was doing, she thought. *He knows if he doesn't say anything, I'll die of curiosity.* That was so unfair.

"You surprised me. I never expected to see you

again, Andy."

"I saw you the day before yesterday on your run. I wasn't sure you'd speak to me."

Aimee paused. Then asked, "So when do you leave for California?"

"I haven't decided yet. Cory's gone to Texas and offered to let me stay in the house for a little bit. I'm supposed to box up his things and send them out to him in exchange."

"So, he's moved there, permanently?"

"It's a year-long training program, if he makes it through. Not everyone does."

Aimee developed a cramp in her side and stopped. She placed her hands on her knees and bent over, taking deep breaths.

Andy stopped as well. "Are you okay?"

She nodded. "Cramp."

Aimee pulled her water bottle out of the back of her fleece running jacket, unscrewed the top and drank several gulps. She handed the bottle to Andy.

His eyes were soft and friendly, the coldness of three days ago gone. It was so unfair how incredibly handsome he was. She watched him drink water, trying not to stare at the way his neck looked when he swallowed, and it made her thirsty too.

"Thanks," he said, handing the bottle back to her. She screwed the top back on and shoved it at her waist behind her, giving him a smirk, intentionally trying not to smile.

She looked at her watch. "Okay, looks like I have about ten minutes and then I'm supposed to turn around and go the other direction. I can go farther if you'd like." She resumed her pace.

"Can I buy you breakfast at Connie's?"

Aimee had practiced what she would say if Andy had tried to call her. But she hadn't been prepared for this.

"I don't know."

"You don't know if you're hungry or you don't know if you want to?" he asked, his voice smooth and level.

"I don't know."

"Are you still angry?"

"Shouldn't I be?"

"It's a choice, Aimee. It's up to you, but I'd still have breakfast with you, even if you are still angry."

She was losing the battle. He was so disarming, letting her completely run the conversation, sticking to her like glue as they continued down the beach. He wasn't going to stop.

"Okay, I give up."

"Just say when."

A few paces later, she pointed off to the left and then walked across the softer sand and up the steps to the beach access trail. They went single file between the buildings with the palm trees over their heads, just like before.

He turned the corner before she did, opening the door for her. She didn't make eye contact, but when they were seated at a table, he sat across from her. She couldn't avoid him any longer.

The plastic menu gave her some cover as she delved into every line, reading everything printed there, even though she knew what she was going to order, would always order.

Their waitress brought over coffee for both of them without asking.

Andy spoke before Aimee could open her mouth.

"We'll have two thirty-fives, with slices of avocado on the side. You can put the potatoes on my plate. One order of biscuits, please, no gravy."

She was shocked.

"Tell me, honestly. Don't you think I would remember all that, Aimee?"

His blue eyes were intense, almost dangerous. The question still hung in the air as she studied his face and then had to turn away.

He handed her the half-and-half, which she used and returned to him.

"I'd like to know how you're doing, something other than fine," he said.

Was he mocking her? Making fun of something she did?

"I've been staying busy. I've kept up the running and been busy with—" she didn't want to mention the house or that she was close to locating her brother— "I've gotten caught up in my reading."

He picked up the flaky biscuit, halved it with his knife, buttered both halves lavishly, and handed her the bottom side.

She pressed it carefully between her thumb and fingers and then took a big bite out of it, closing her eyes at the orgasmic taste and texture of the thing. When she opened her eyes, Andy had stopped eating and was staring back at her.

"How about you?"

"I took Cory to the airport yesterday early. Stopped by the grocery store. Oh, and I did some laundry and called my LPO back home.

"You think this will be a good thing for Cory to do?"

"He had good instincts on that one. It was his execution that was lacking."

A warm ripple of pain washed over her, and then was gone. "I try not to think about it," she whispered.

Their omelets arrived, and Aimee found her appetite had kicked into overdrive.

Andy held up the other biscuit and she shook her

head no.

"He wanted to make sure you knew he'd gone there, made it."

Aimee picked away at the fresh crab piled on the top of her eggs. He was still watching her.

"Look, Andy, just what is this?"

"This is breakfast. Did I do something wrong?"

"You're looking at me too much."

He dropped his fork and sat back in his chair, finally releasing a short smile.

"What?" she asked.

"Can I ask you a question?"

"I'm not sure. You're being weird."

"I'm going to ask you anyway." He waited until she looked up at him.

"Go ahead."

"Are you intending to get back together with Cory?"

"Oh, that's an easy one. Absolutely not. I wish him all the luck, but with the talk about other women? I just go dead inside when I hear that. I don't wish him any ill will, but he's a stranger to me now."

"Then would you consider being my friend, perhaps a little more?"

Instantly she blushed. She nearly spit out her eggs.

"You tell me," she struggled to say. "Why should I consider this? Besides, you guys have this code that you don't—"

"I can't stop thinking about you, Aimee."

She scrambled to her feet, attempting to break for the door. He was there in an instant, held her by her forearms, and then gently folded her into his chest. She took two seconds of enjoyment, and then stiffened and pulled away.

"This is insane. You are insane. This is not happening."

"Are you done?" he asked, pointing to the table.

"Yes."

He threw down some money, put his arm around her shoulder, and led her outside.

"Look, Andy. I'm sorry. You ruined your breakfast. I feel bad about that."

He put his hands on her shoulders and steered her through the palm-studded path.

"I made a mistake, that's all. I should be the one who's sorry."

Aimee ached she was so uncomfortable. Why?

Neither one of them began running. They walked at a leisurely pace close to the water's edge, until they came to Cory's house. He was about to wave, or extend a hand for her to shake, when she suddenly realized something.

"Andy, I have some clothes there. Would you mind if I got them today?"

"Sure. No problem. Do you have a lot of things?"

"I honestly don't remember."

"I've got some boxes. We can see, and if it's too much to carry, I can drop them by your house later on, if you like."

"Could you drive me home this morning?"

"Sure, that works too."

The ghost of Cory loomed large once she was inside. She tiptoed, as if she was going to wake him, into the bedroom, and collected some underwear from a drawer, along with some jeans and a sweatshirt. She found a couple pairs of socks, her toothbrush, some face wash, and a brush in the bathroom.

In the living room, she found two books. Everything she had fit into one box with room to spare.

Andy had made coffee, and he presented her with a mug, filled with cream. He clinked his mug against hers.

"Friends?"

"Friends," she repeated and gulped her coffee.

Aimee walked to the window to admire the view, as she always had in this little place. Andy sat on the back of the couch behind her.

She was on the edge of so much right now. Maybe she was going to find Logan. Maybe she'd find out about the pink house. Was she ready to let someone else in as well? Was she ready to share? And what if it didn't work out?

She'd done it before, and she was still standing. Her life was going to go on almost without missing a beat. Nothing was ever without risk. There were always unforeseen consequences. Cory hadn't been the man she thought he was. She knew that even before she learned about all his secrets.

But Andy, she'd liked him from the first day she met him. And right now, he was offering an invitation she knew she'd regret not taking.

Aimee took one last drink of her warm creamy coffee, set the mug down on the bookshelf next to the window, and walked over to him. She was so close that she felt the heat of his body. Their eyes locked as she removed the cup from his fingers, placing it next to hers on the bookshelf.

He continued to wait for her. She approached again, this time touching his face with her fingertips and running a forefinger across his lips. She looked into his eyes one last time, inhaled, and pressed her lips then her whole body against his.

Two powerful arms wrapped around her back, then slid lower to her buttocks, which he pressed into his groin. He gasped and pulled her up so her legs could wrap around his hips. With quick steps, he carried her into the guest bedroom.

Their undressing was slow with attention to every

kiss, every bare spot that demanded to be touched, kissed, or tasted. She removed her snug running pants and stood before him naked.

He kneeled before her, parting her thighs and kissed her from her knees to the soft tissues of her sex. He sat down on the edge of the bed and pulled her to him, and then slowly, he moved backward onto the soft mattress, and with one arm wrapped tightly around her waist, brought her with him.

The sheets held his scent. He was careful to tuck her beneath him. She wrapped one leg up around his hip as he climbed her body, kissing he navel, and then working up to her neck, and lastly, her lips. She held his cock while they kissed, and then with long stroking motions, positioned him to take her. The length of him filled her, every inch. Her pulse quickened as he pulled out, and then lunged forward, deeper still, his lips sucking on her earlobe with the diamond stud in it.

His hips were fluid and gentle as he rocked her world, pleasuring her, changing angles, turning her over and taking her from behind. She followed his hands, her fingers entwined between his, to feel what he was feeling, touch and pinch where he touched and pinched. His hot tongue lit her on fire. She bit his earlobe and pulled at his hair when at last her climax was full upon her. He answered her pleasure with his own, holding her as tightly as she clutched him, stopping so she could feel the power of his pulse inside her. They remained entangled, limbs and sheets, until the spasms subsided.

She was right. There was no predicting where all this would lead.

All she knew was that she wanted more.

CHAPTER 17

Andy could not believe that their connection was so complete, like they'd been lovers for years. He didn't want to stop. He could have stayed in bed all day. He knew she had things she'd planned on doing today, but they couldn't help but explore, fondle, kiss, and taste each other, savoring each delight and morsel, resting, and then starting all over again.

He lay in the noonday light and marveled at the shadows that played along the peach colors of her smooth spine, the gentle curve of it, the dimples above her butt cheeks, and the deep, dark places he could find when he slid his fingers down her belly. He'd never worshiped a woman so thoroughly. Every time he came inside her, he wanted to give her more.

She rolled over on her back, her forearm shielding the light from her eyes. He suckled on her right breast, bringing her nipple to a stiff peak, twisting it between his thumb and fingers until she arched up.

He pulled her limp body over his and felt her heart beating and the pleasure of her pubic bone grinding into his thigh, begging for him to plunder her again. She whimpered as he ran his fingers over her breasts, complaining that they ached. Her body wanted him even though her sex was swollen and bright pink. It drove him crazy that she was hairless in all those places he wanted full access to.

Flipping her over, he pulled her hips up and inserted a pillow beneath her tummy. His finger traced down her spine, over the cleft in her buttocks, down to where her swollen, glistening sex called to him. Her taste was exquisite. His tongue thrust deep, causing her to moan into her pillow, arch her back, and present her rear to him so perfectly.

Her taste had driven him crazy, making him rock hard. It wasn't fair she couldn't see what a beautiful sight it was to enter her from behind, spreading her fleshy cheeks as his hands kneaded them, his fingers bit into them as he rammed himself deep inside her.

Again, she moaned, and it made him harder and bigger still.

At last, he rode her, the pace quickening urgently, their thighs slapping against each other with every stroke. She pressed against him Her internal muscles milked his cock, clamped down on him tight. He felt her spasm. Her breaths gasped as she squeezed the sheets and screamed when her long, rolling orgasm washed over her, fully taking control.

He cooled the little warm beads of sweat on her spine by blowing on her. He brought her a cool washrag for her violated sex.

He whispered in her ear, "I wanted to let you sleep, Aimee, but I'm so sorry. I just couldn't."

She giggled. He pulled her hair from her face and smiled.

"Go ahead and get a little rest, but," he said as he kissed her soft behind, "no promises, okay?"

She moaned something, her eyelashes slowly moving up and down, and then she was asleep.

THEY AWOKE AGAIN in the early afternoon. Cory's shower was almost too small for the both of them, but they managed to soap each other off. He shampooed her hair, and she did his. As they were rinsed off, sluicing the soapy goodness down their bodies, he took her again, pressing her soft body against the cool shower tiles.

And, after another soaping off, they finally stepped out. The water had gone completely cold.

She changed into clothes she'd left behind. He opened some soup and made a green salad.

"So I have news about my brother."

"Really?" Andy was surprised.

"It was him who I saw at the restaurant, remember, JJ's? Remember, that night, I thought I saw him. I went back there yesterday and talked to the manager, and the bookkeeper. He came from a halfway house, and I've got the name and address."

"Do you want to go over there today?"

"That was the plan, originally." She blushed.

"I'm glad we did this."

"Me too," she said and kissed him.

She pulled the picture of her brother from her wallet and then showed him the address of the facility.

THE SUNSHINE PALMS appeared to be part of an old Florida office building at one time. It was tucked away in a forest of jungle foliage with a canopy of tall palm trees. The entrance of the center had an elegant lake, populated by a dozen pink flamingos.

It looked expensive.

"How did he manage to get in here?"

"I have no idea. Everything about my brother is a mystery to me."

At the reception area, a man in white uniform greeted them. Andy wasn't sure if he was security, or a health employee.

"Can I help you?"

"I'm looking for my brother. He disappeared from our home about seven years ago. I was recently told he was at this address."

"You have to be on the approved medical file list for next of kin. You have a name so I can check?"

"Logan Greer." Aimee added, "I have this family photograph, which shows him ten years ago." She passed the picture over the counter to him, along with her driver's license.

The receptionist typed in the computer then returned both the drivers' license and the photograph. "I'm sorry, ma'am, but we don't have anyone at this facility by that name. Could he go by any other name?"

"How about the counselors? Could we speak to one of them? I know he'd identify as someone else. We've tried to find him for so long, and as of last week, he took a job through his treatment here. Somebody must have seen him."

"In order to protect our patients, we don't let people inside unless it's recommended by a doctor."

Andy decided to step in. "Look, sir, she's just trying to find her brother. We'd like access to your staff and counselors, because he was sent from here to his job at JJ's, where he was last Wednesday. Can't we circulate the picture around and see someone?"

The attendant darted glances between the two of them.

"Why don't you have a seat in the lobby? I'll make a call and see what I can do. Just wait a few minutes over there," he said as he pointed to two red leather loveseats facing one another.

Aimee tried to listen to what was being said on the phone but without luck. He spoke to another party and then, ended the call with, "All right. I'll tell them. Thank you."

He approached. "If you'll follow me, I'm going to show you to the small conference room. Dr. Denby is going to see you."

"Thank you," whispered Aimee, suddenly heartened.

The conference room was anything but small. The conference table was made from the interior slice of a very large tree, the gnarly edges polished with clear coating. The tabletop itself varied in color from a golden amber in the center to darker and darker rings of brown radiating out, ending at the rough edges.

Aimee set her purse down, leaving the head of the table for someone else.

Andy sat next to her.

"Can I bring you some water?" the attendant asked.

"Please, two," answered Andy.

Dr. Denby was next to enter, carrying the two waters. Andy stood, shaking the doctor's hand. Aimee stayed seated and did the same.

"Thanks for this," she said, holding up the bottle.

He had pure white hair, worn long enough that it

curled a bit at his collar. The top of his head was smooth and perfectly brushed, with every hair in place. His hands were marked with age spots and wrinkled, but his face was remarkably youthful.

"So what can I do for you two today? You have a missing relative you're trying to find?"

"Yes, my brother," Aimee said as she showed him the family picture. "That's him," she said as she pointed to Logan.

He squinted, angling the photo and then looking at the back side. He pushed it back to Aimee with his forefinger.

"What's this boy's name?" He got out his pen and produced a small spiral notebook from his white lab coat pocket.

"Logan Greer. This picture was taken about ten years ago. When we both were in high school."

He wrote Logan's name on the tablet, then the number ten, and underlined it.

"And how did you happen to come here?"

"I saw him last week at JJ's restaurant, you know, at Indian Rocks Beach?"

"You talked to him?"

"Not exactly. I saw him out in the parking lot. He was arguing with someone, and when I called out his name, he disappeared. I went back yesterday to ask about him and was told your center helps people with problems get jobs. She wouldn't give me any details, of course, but gave me this address. That's why we're here. I was told he'd been fired. I was wondering if he'd been placed somewhere else."

The doctor continued making notes and then added a period and set down his pen.

"I take it you are aware of his problem with drugs and alcohol?"

"Oh yes. My parents had him in rehab several times. It nearly bankrupted them."

"I hear that story a lot in these rooms. It's a very sad fact of life here."

"So can we see him?"

"Unfortunately, he's not here now. Even if he were, I'd have to get his permission. But in answer to your original question, I believe I helped with this boy's rehabilitation during his stay here. But he didn't tell us about having a sibling, or parents. And he didn't go by the name Logan Greer."

"What name did he use?" Andy asked.

The doctor looked toward the ceiling, trying to recall. "Ben Hawkins, I believe it was. Yes. Ben." He stared back down at the photo. "I'm afraid he didn't look like that, but I can see it is Ben."

"What do you mean?" Aimee asked.

"You have to understand, when we get homeless on an outreach fellowship, they often have advanced cases of mental disease, along with whatever other issues caused by their addictions. But years of abusing themselves makes them age, and of course, it wears on the body."

"So did he get transferred somewhere else?" Aimee asked.

"No, he was placed with that job, as I understand it, and a bed at a halfway house within walking distance to the restaurant, since they don't usually have a car. Apparently, he was caught stealing alcohol and was terminated. And then, he just walked away. Disappeared."

"That's exactly what he did to my parents."

"That's all so tragic. I have several parents' groups formed to discuss that very thing. It's heartbreaking."

Andy leaned forward to ask his question.

"What did you mean when you said *outreach fellowship*?"

"We are governed by a Board of Directors for a nonprofit foundation. Our charter stipulates that we reserve five beds at all times for the indigent or homeless, as long as they aren't a danger to the other patients. You would call them paying customers, I suppose."

"So how did he get here?" Andy asked.

"I'd have to get Ben's file, but most of them come from Emergency Rooms, an accidental overdose, or the police find them in parks. Sometimes an encampment is raided, and they distribute several of the homeless to various church groups, the Rescue Mission, and other clinics like ours. There are some state-run treatment centers, but most of them are filled up with criminal cases."

"So it was random, then?" Aimee asked.

"Yes. I don't know how they do it. Maybe someone thought he needed a break. I'd have to look at his record to tell you that."

"So where do you suggest she look next?" Andy asked.

Dr. Denby clasped his hands together on the shiny wooden conference table. "I don't think he can be found, because I don't think he wants to be."

Aimee felt like he'd slapped her across the face. She'd been so hopeful.

"I'll bet you're thinking I'm being quite harsh, but actually, I'm trying to help. The reality of the situation is that homelessness is a huge problem now, and we don't have enough facilities to deal with it. Many of them self-medicate. They try to monitor the underlying mental components of their disease, which in turn, deepens the cycle. They become more and more aloof and eventually get in harm's way or lose their connection to reality altogether. If you saw him on the street today, I'd recommend not engaging him or trying to help him. You'd be putting yourself in danger, in my opinion."

Aimee began to cry.

Dr. Denby placed his hand over Aimee's. "I'm so sorry, child. I wish I had better news for you. But you could devote all your time and all your money to trying to find and rehabilitate this boy, and he'd run back to the streets at the first opportunity. He may be alive, but he's not living."

"When he was released to the halfway house, was he well?"

Dr. Denby withdrew his hand from Aimee's. "Oh, we never get the well ones!" He chuckled. "Occasionally, someone gets out and breaks the cycle. Most of them fail. Although we talk about homelessness in one broad tent, it's not a one-size-fits-all type of problem. And we're not even scratching the surface. Every state, every municipality, treats it differently and with varying success. The worst thing we can do is what we are doing: Basically nothing."

Aimee didn't try to hide her tears any longer.

"This is the worst part of my job, bringing the reality of addiction to the very people who want to hang on to every hope. But like I said before, I think that's cruel."

Andy nodded, putting his arm around Aimee. "You have any other questions, sweetheart?"

All she could do was shake her head no.

Dr. Denby stood up, and Andy did the same. They shook hands again, and then the doctor placed his hand on Aimee's shoulder. "It's healthy that you care. That's the normal response. You suffer because you understand the truth. You feel pain because you're a good person, compassionate and generous, or else you'd never be here. Make sure you continue to bring that to the world, but I don't think you can fix this one, no matter how much you want to. Okay, Aimee?"

She nodded her head again and pulled herself up.

"Thank you, doctor," she mumbled.

Dr. Denby smiled for the first time. "I've flagged the file and will add your phone number, if you'll write it here." He pushed his notebook in front of her and set his pen down next to it. "If I hear anything at all, I'll be sure to call you. I can do that."

Aimee wrote her number down and handed back his pen. He walked to the doorway and held it open.

"Here's another tip that works well for some people." Both Aimee and Andy quickly looked up to his face. "Go some place you love being. Walk the beach, and remember him the way he was. Go have an ice cream as if you were sharing it with him." he said with a timid smile.

Aimee felt crippled. Her heart hurt. She was so sure she could find Logan. She'd anticipated sitting in his room, talking to him, catching up as if they'd been separated at college or long trips. He'd make her laugh. He'd play drums with pencils on every surface of her bedroom. Make her dolls talk. Peek out the window and tell her there was a dinosaur outside eating her mother's roses. The best parts of her childhood were with Logan.

How could she give up?

Andy took her hand while they walked to the Jeep.

"Sunshine Palms, what a depressing place. Why don't they just call it the Gates of Hell?"

Andy threw his arm around her, squeezed, and brought her in tight. "There's that pretty girl with the lavender eyes who's got me all tied up in knots."

"Are you suggesting?" She looked up at him, wiggling her eyebrows up and down.

"No worries, no rush. We've got time. I'm rather enjoying the getting acquainted part. Aren't you?"

She chuckled. "Roger that."

"Your chariot awaits," he said as he opened the door and hoisted her up into the passenger seat. "Where to?"

"I *don't* feel like ice cream," she said. "I want to think about something else." She wiped her cheeks with the backs of her hands. "I want to show you something near my house. Take me there, okay?"

"Anything, Aimee. Anything you want."

CHAPTER 18

ANDY HELD HER hand all the way up the coast until he turned down the alleyway toward the shore and the gravel driveway in front of Aimee's house. She'd been watching the little beach shops, eateries and Gator Golf stands as they whizzed by them. Her window was ajar, and the wind blew against her face, sending her light caramel hair in all directions.

Instead of going inside, she took his hand and led him down the Beach Access bridge and then turned south and walked in the soft sand in front of several houses. She stopped at a two-story rose-colored home with a huge balcony overlooking the ocean. All the windows were boarded up. She led him around the right side of the house, opening up a door and then through a windowless storage area and through another door to a kitchen of sorts.

The place was a total mess. Appliances looked like big, angular dead animals on the killing fields. A sliver of light enabled him to see a large wraparound counter and eating bar, tiled in vintage pink ceramic with black trim. She stepped carefully, avoiding broken glass and sharp metal pieces, leading him to a stairway with half the wooden spindles missing. She danced halfway up before Andy began.

Old furniture lay broken, and both bathrooms were missing toilets, vanity tops and shower heads. The master at the end had a sliding glass door, leading to the balcony. Aimee kicked a piece of plywood out, giving them a space to walk out on the deck.

"Careful, Aimee. I'm not sure this is solid." He was going to lead her away from the railing but examined the timbers below their feet.

"Look at that view!" she said, turning to face the now-dying sun. "I'll bet you get an extra two minutes of sunset with this balcony," she said.

People in clumps of two or three began to gather, everyone watching the same direction, as if getting nourishment from the sun's rays themselves.

"Pretty spectacular, I'll admit."

He watched her stand on her tip-toes, hanging on the railing for extra height.

"Careful, Aimee. I don't think that wood is very sturdy." He pulled her back. She turned, facing him, her eyes sparkling.

"What do you think, Andy. Should I buy it?"

"Buy it? You have a house."

"That I rent. What if I were to buy it?"

Andy noticed she hadn't said anything about him being part of that picture. "You want to live here full time?"

"Why not?"

He remained quiet and hoped that she'd self-correct a mistake he thought she made.

"Is it for sale?"

"I looked up the owner's name. It's left in a trust for the benefit of a lady who lives in Sarasota in one of those senior communities. I'm going to contact the attorney and see. Don't you love it?"

"It's broken. It needs a lot of work. Who—?"

She placed her palm over his mouth to stop him. Then she kissed him. "Would you help me?

"Well, you do remember that I live in California? Aimee, it would be hard to see each other very much if we were looking at two sunsets from different coasts. Right?"

"I thought about that. But you could help me find the contractors to do the work, maybe help me get organized. And I can stay here while you're on deployment."

The part that was missing was having her lined up with all the other parents, kids, wives, and girlfriends when their big transport came booming into town. Her being present at the bonfires and parties, walking with her through the shops in Coronado, having pizza and beers with some of his friends and their ladies at the Scupper. There was a whole life there, in San Diego, that he loved and didn't want to give up.

She was focusing on the last embers of the sun spilling into the ocean. In an instant, the sky and colors of everything began to gray and tone down.

She crossed in front of him. "Come on. We better get out of here before we can't see."

They silently traversed back until they were at the side of the house again. "I like the color, at least."

Her expression was smug, unreadable.

"Let's go to the Crab Shack, okay? I'm still going through withdrawals from this morning."

Even though it was early still for the dinner hour, the restaurant was nearly filled to capacity. There was a singer playing Margaritaville songs and taking requests. He tipped his hat at Aimee, but she didn't notice.

They sat up front, away from the music by her choice.

The waitress took Aimee's order of a strawberry margarita. Andy stuck to beer.

The way she sucked on her straw brought back some very sexy memories of this morning. She apparently knew it, because she let her tongue slip up the straw and back down again. Her eyes were dreamy, slightly out of focus. She stared right at him and licked her lips.

"I thought you wanted to eat tonight," he said.

"Promises, promises."

That little statement and the fact that her tongue completely coated her lips made his pants feel two sizes too small. She gave him a long, vacant look as she put the straw between her lips and sucked. Hard.

Andy had to look away.

The waitress arrived, and before she could mention the specials, Aimee ordered for both of them.

"He's going to have the breaded, barbeque oysters, a dozen, and we'll share a king crab legs special."

"Nothing healthy?" he asked. Andy had expected a salad they could share at least.

"This is healthy. Can't you feel it?" She grinned.

He knew how to change the subject. It wasn't that he didn't want to partake. He was starved for real food.

"So tell me about your plans for that pink house. Tell me how you're going to get a loan on that place in its present condition."

"I don't know what they want yet, but I plan to pay cash and do the remodel for cash as well. I can get a loan later, if I want."

"I was hoping you'd come with me to San Diego. Soon, Aimee. Or is this a little wrinkle, a change of plans. Or did I misunderstand?" He felt his voice trail off, having trouble following where the conversation was going.

"You think I demonstrated any desire to take a detour this morning?"

"No, you certainly did not."

"Did I demonstrate a lack of enthusiasm?"

"Not one bit. I loved every moan, whimper, and….you fill in the blanks."

"Oh, trust me. I can," she purred.

"I'm rather counting on it. But seriously, honey, are we talking about a long-distance romance here, because I was rather sure I'd convinced you I wanted you with me twenty-four-seven."

"I want that too. But what if we had a special place at Sunset Beach to come? What if we owned it for years and years and years? What if we became like those older couples on the beach, and we watch the young ones, like we are right now, scampering home to do whatever? We could rent it out. Share our beach with other people and make a little money at it. We could share it with friends or give it as a gift for a week or two. Then our Sunset Beach would blow up and take over our whole lives. It would be bigger, better than just the private place where we met and…fill in the blanks."

"Fell in love."

"That's what I want, Andy. I want something that will never go away."

"You know what I do. That could still happen."

"But I'd have you here, always. You'd always be here with me, no matter what the age, where you were. This is for *us*."

The crab legs arrived and took up the entire table. A pint of melted butter was delivered in a Mason jar. Andy's oysters were tucked into the far corner, with barely room for his beer or her margarita.

"This is totally obscene!" he said.

"I'm going to be covered in butter," she said.

"One of my favorite flavors." He slid the first two oysters into his mouth and called them perfect. Aimee tried one as well.

She tilted her head. "An acquired taste but good."

She dove into the largest of the legs, pulling off the pre-cracked portions easily and dipping them into butter with her fingers. She fed him. He fed her another oyster.

When they were done, shells and small pools of butter were everywhere, covering the tabletop, even falling at their feet below. She finished her margarita.

She had her head in her palm, elbow resting on the table.

"I love your idea. I'm all on board. Let's make it happen, Aimee."

MONTHS LATER, WHEN they would think about this night, he would tell people that he knew the first time he saw her that he would make her his wife. That he never asked her and she never consented with words. They said their vows all night long, this time in her bed. It didn't matter how long they'd known each other, because their forever began with the first kiss and the number thirty-five omelet at Connie's.

It was all about the butter, the crab, and the beautiful Florida night air.

And the sunsets that would last for all eternity at Sunset Beach.

Continue the journey to Sunset Beach with Book 2 of this new series, Second Chance SEAL (The Girl He Left Behind), releasing in March. You can order it here.

Navy SEAL Damon Hamblin's life is in turmoil after he's served with divorce papers during his last deployment. He crashes into a sleepy Florida Gulf Coast town to drown his sorrows and just fade into the background, where no one knows him and he can drink, surf and lay out on the beach until his insides heal. The last thing he wants is to rebound into another relationship.

Martel Long came to Sunset Beach five years ago to visit a friend, and never left. She's tried to forget the man who broke her heart back home, and had been doing a good job of it, until she comes face to face with him at a Bachelorette party for her best friend at a local beach bar.

As sparks fly and old wounds are torn open, the sands at Sunset Beach help to heal a beautiful love story that could have been, and will be again.

ABOUT THE AUTHOR

NYT and USA Today best-selling author Sharon Hamilton's award-winning Navy SEAL Brotherhood series have been a fan favorite from the day the first one was released. They've earned her the coveted Amazon author ranking of #1 in Romantic Suspense, Military Romance and Contemporary Romance categories, as well as in Gothic Romance for her Vampires of Tuscany and Guardian Angels. Her characters follow a sometimes rocky road to redemption through passion and true love.

Now that he's out of the Navy, Sharon can share with her readers that her son spent a decade as a Navy SEAL, and he's the inspiration for her books.

Her Golden Vampires of Tuscany are not like any vamps you've read about before, since they don't go to ground and can walk around in the full light of the sun.

Her Guardian Angels struggle with the human charges they are sent to save, often escaping their vanilla world of Heaven for the brief human one. You won't find any of these beings in any Sunday school class.

She lives in Sonoma County, California with her husband and her Doberman, Tucker. A lifelong organic gardener, when she's not writing, she's getting *verra verra* dirty in the mud, or wandering Farmers Markets looking for new Heirloom varieties of vegetables and flowers. She and her husband plan to cure their wanderlust (or make it worse) by traveling in their Diesel Class A Pusher, Romance Rider. Starting with this book, all her writing will be done on the road.

She loves hearing from her fans:
Sharonhamilton2001@gmail.com

Her website is:
sharonhamiltonauthor.com

Find out more about Sharon, her upcoming releases, appearances and news when you sign up for Sharon's newsletter.

Facebook:
facebook.com/SharonHamiltonAuthor

Twitter:
twitter.com/sharonlhamilton

Pinterest:
pinterest.com/AuthorSharonH

Amazon:
amazon.com/Sharon-Hamilton/e/B004FQQMAC

BookBub:
bookbub.com/authors/sharon-hamilton

Youtube:
youtube.com/channel/UCDInkxXFpXp_4Vnq08ZxMBQ

Soundcloud:
soundcloud.com/sharon-hamilton-1

Sharon Hamilton's Rockin' Romance Readers:
facebook.com/groups/sealteamromance

Sharon Hamilton's Goodreads Group:
goodreads.com/group/show/199125-sharon-hamilton-readers-group

Visit Sharon's Online Store:
sharon-hamilton-author.myshopify.com

Join Sharon's Review Teams:

eBook Reviews:
sharonhamiltonassistant@gmail.com

Audio Reviews:
sharonhamiltonassistant@gmail.com

Life is one fool thing after another.
Love is two fool things after each other.

REVIEWS

PRAISE FOR THE
GOLDEN VAMPIRES OF TUSCANY SERIES

"Well to say the least I was thoroughly surprise. I have read many Vampire books, from Ann Rice to Kym Grosso and few other Authors, so yes I do like Vampires, not the super scary ones from the old days, but the new ones are far more interesting far more human then one can remember. I found Honeymoon Bite a totally engrossing book, I was not able to put it down, page after page I found delight, love, understanding, well that is until the bad bad Vamp started being really bad. But seeing someone love another person so much that they would do anything to protect them, well that had me going, then well there was more and for a while I thought it was the end of a beautiful love story that spanned not only time but, spanned Italy and California. Won't divulge how it ended, but I did shed a few tears after screaming but Sharon Hamilton did not let me down, she took me on amazing trip that I loved, look forward to reading another Vampire book of hers."

"An excellent paranormal romance that was exciting, romantic, entertaining and very satisfying to read. It had me anticipating what would happen next many times over, so much so I could not put it down and even finished it up in a day. The vampires in this book were different from your average vampire, but I enjoy different variations and changes to the same old stuff. It made for a more unpredictable read and more adventurous to explore! Vampire lovers, any paranormal readers and even those who love the romance genre will enjoy Honeymoon Bite."

"This is the first non-Seal book of this author's I have read and I loved it. There is a cast-like hierarchy in this vampire community with humans at the very bottom and Golden vampires at the top. Lionel is a dark vampire who are servants of the Goldens. Phoebe is a Golden who has not decided if she will remain human or accept the turning to become a vampire. Either way she and Lionel can never be together since it is forbidden.

I enjoyed this story and I am looking forward to the next installment."

"A hauntingly romantic read. Old love lost and new love found. Family, heart, intrigue and vampires. Grabbed my attention and couldn't put down. Would definitely recommend."

PRAISE FOR THE
SEAL BROTHERHOOD SERIES

"Fans of Navy SEAL romance, I found a new author to feed your addiction. Finely written and loaded delicious with moments, Sharon Hamilton's storytelling satisfies like a thick bar of chocolate." —Marliss Melton, bestselling author of the *Team Twelve* Navy SEALs series

"Sharon Hamilton does an EXCELLENT job of fitting all the characters into a brotherhood of SEALS that may not be real but sure makes you feel that you have entered the circle and security of their world. The stories intertwine with each book before…and each book after and THAT is what makes Sharon Hamilton's SEAL Brotherhood Series so very interesting. You won't want to put down ANY of her books and they will keep you reading into the night when you should be sleeping. Start with this book…and you will not want to stop until you've read the whole series and then…you will be waiting for Sharon to write the next one." (5 Star Review)

"Kyle and Christy explode all over the pages in this first book, *[Accidental SEAL],* in a whole new series of SEALs. If the twist and turns don't get your heart jumping, then maybe the suspense will. This is a must read for those that are looking for love and adventure with a little sloppy love thrown in for good measure." (5 Star Review)

PRAISE FOR THE
BAD BOYS OF SEAL TEAM 3 SERIES

"I love reading this series! Once you start these books, you can hardly put them down. The mix of romance and suspense keeps you turning the pages one right after another! Can't wait until the next book!" (5 Star Review)

"I love all of Sharon's Seal books, but *[SEAL's Code]* may just be her best to date. Danny and Luci's journey is filled with a wonderful insight into the Native American life. It is a love story that will fill you with warmth and contentment. You will enjoy Danny's journey to become a SEAL and his reasons for it. Good job Sharon!" (5 Star Review)

PRAISE FOR THE
BAND OF BACHELORS SERIES

"*[Lucas]* was the first book in the Band of Bachelors series and it was a phenomenal start. I loved how we got to see the other SEALs we all love and we got a look at Lucas and Marcy. They had an instant attraction, and their love was very intense. This book had it all, suspense, steamy romance, humor, everything you want in a riveting, outstanding read. I can't wait to read the next book in this series." (5 Star Review)

PRAISE FOR THE
TRUE BLUE SEALS SERIES

"Keep the tissues box nearby as you read *True Blue SEALs: Zak* by Sharon Hamilton. I imagine more than I wish to that the circumstances surrounding Zak and Amy are all too real for returning military personnel and their families. Ms. Hamilton has put us right in the middle of struggles and successes that these two high school sweethearts endure. I have read several of Sharon Hamilton's military romances but will say this is the most emotionally intense of the ones that I have read. This is a well-written, realistic story with authentic characters that will have you rooting for them and proud of those who serve to keep us safe. This is an author who writes amazing stories that you love and cry with the characters. Fans of Jessica Scott and Marliss Melton will want to add Sharon Hamilton to their list of realistic military romance writers." (5 Star Review)

"Dear FATHER IN HEAVEN,

If I may respectfully say so sometimes you are a strange God. Though you love all mankind,

It seems you have special predilections too.

You seem to love those men who can stand up alone who face impossible odds, Who challenge every bully and every tyrant ~

Those men who know the heat and loneliness of Calvary. Possibly you cherish men of this stamp because you recognize the mark of your only son in them.

Since this unique group of men known as the SEALs know Calvary and suffering, teach them now the mystery of the resurrection ~ that they are indestructible, that they will live forever because of their deep faith in you.

And when they do come to heaven, may I respectfully warn you, Dear Father, they also know how to celebrate. So please be ready for them when they insert under your pearly gates.

Bless them, their devoted Families and their Country on this glorious occasion.

We ask this through the merits of your Son, Christ Jesus the Lord, Amen."

> By Reverend E.J. McMalhon S.J. LCDR, CHC, USN
> Awards Ceremony SEAL Team One
> 1975 At NAB, Coronado

Made in the USA
Monee, IL
12 May 2020